THE PERSIAN Prince AND THE HAN Princess

—— THE PERSIAN PRINCE BOOK II ——

JACK A. TAYLOR

THE PERSIAN

Prince

AND THE HAN

Princess

—— THE PERSIAN PRINCE BOOK II ——

THE PERSIAN PRINCE AND THE HAN PRINCESS
Copyright © 2025 by Jack A. Taylor

ISBN: 978-1-4866-2564-2
eBook ISBN: 978-1-4866-2565-9

Word Alive Press
119 De Baets Street Winnipeg, MB R2J 3R9
www.wordalivepress.ca

WORD ALIVE
—P R E S S—

Cataloguing in Publication information can be obtained from Library and Archives Canada.

To all who dare to cross cultures, barriers, and dreams to overcome their fears, their limits, and the expectations that hold them back. To all who are willing to fight for love to the ends of the world and back.

One

The Way is the way.

Not everyone knew that.

Ardeshir wiped the sweat off his bald dark head and itched the chin under his curly black goatee with the back of his hand.

The secluded grounds of the Han emperor were warmer than his home in Persia. A flock of honking bar-headed geese, migrating from their flight over the Himalayas, landed on the emperor's pond with a flurry of wings. The pale grey honkers scrambled out of the water and grazed on the short grass. A pair of swans, usually occupying the pond, sheltered under willow branches away from the noisy visitors.

Yes. The Way is the way. Balance. Truth. Hope. Life. Light.

Ardeshir paced the bamboo floor and weighed the words on his tongue. First, in his native Farsi. Second, in his acquired Mandarin. If he could only prove himself here, his father might smile on him again.

He fumbled through the line again. If he didn't prove himself, would he be welcomed back home?

"The Way is the way."

Balanced. Like the blend of his skin between dark and light. Like the blend of Persian poetry and Oriental song-chants. Like the blend of color on the blue-tailed bee-eater resting on a willow near the emperor's garden pond.

With a bow toward the hemp paper treasuring his precious thoughts, he laid down his quill and drank in the scene. As if in response, sunrays burst through the rumbling storm clouds over the mountain peaks and bathed the emperor's red-tiled palace in brilliance. If only he could get an audience with that elusive icon of power and complete his mission and message. Then he could get back home to his family in Susa.

The gardener had assured him that all things had their seasons; if he would wait and prove his worthiness, even the simplest soul might catch the eye of the all-seeing one. His own father, Nabonidus, had released him with precious resources to secure silk and treasure to support the farm.

He sighed, the weight of the firstborn resting fully on his shoulders.

If only he could sit alone with the words of life and think on them. The world outside was harsh and evil. His own father had suffered as a gladiator under Rome and a pawn between the Elamite regent and Parthian magi in Persia. All he desired was to reflect on the rainbow that hovered over the pond.

Movement interrupted his internal quest as the geese took wing. A young woman crept nimbly through the emperor's garden toward the pond. It was the emperor's daughter. Her black hair, fastened in a tightly wound nest on her head, sported a yellow chrysanthemum, the symbol of longevity. She glanced over her shoulder and then dashed toward a small boat secured to the dock. Without hesitation she clambered aboard, almost tipping it. She unleashed the rope and took up a paddle.

When she reached the center of the pond, she stopped and sat still as a lotus flower on a breezeless day. A pair of snow-white trumpeter swans glided to the vessel and also stilled.

An irresistible pull on his soul drew his footsteps toward the small grove at the edge of the pond. Hidden, he drank in the sight.

With perfect grace, the goddess before him rose and stood on one foot, absorbing the sunshine. Both her hands were folded as if in prayer. All was well.

She reached into her robe and withdrew an elegant bone flute. The melody arising through her lips was the song of gods and men alike.

And then a carp breached the water and flopped into the boat. With a squeal and windmill of flailing arms, the formerly placid woman flopped into the pond.

Her flailing continued as Ardeshir shed his robe and dove into the water. He reached the distressed woman moments after she was dragged under by the weight of her clothing. He dove under, caught her arm, and dragged her to the surface. Her dark eyes were wild with panic as she gasped for breath; they fixed on him as she continued to flail and beat on him.

"Flute! Flute!" she called out.

"Princess, I am here," he said. "You are safe. Let me take you to land."

This crude effort at Mandarin was enough to make her relax. He set his palm against her spine and helped her float on her back as he guided her to shore. The yellow chrysanthemum drifted away.

Near the edge of the pond, the princess struggled to stand and he released her.

Suddenly, a dozen guardians of the emperor thrashed into the water, some grabbing the princess and others beating on Ardeshir. One guard grabbed his neck and shoved his face into the dirt at the bottom of the pond. He fought as he hoped his father would fight and then chose stillness.

He awoke naked, cold, and alone in darkness. There were no swans, no pond, no bee-eaters, no music, and no day. He stilled himself against the elements.

Only once, standing outside a Han traditional wedding ceremony, had he heard tones as crisp and clean as those played by the princess. That time, an ensemble of suona, sheng, and gongs had accompanied the dizi.

He recreated the pond scene in his mind and attempted to duplicate the lotus-like calm of the princess in her vessel. The effort fed his soul until a torch broke through the blackness and he was dragged to his feet.

Two burly warriors threw him into a pool to wash him off. When he was done scrubbing himself, the two hauled him before a pair of maidens who massaged him, perfumed him, and dressed him in silk robes. Another plaited his hair into a ponytail and laid out sandals for his feet.

Throughout the process, not a word was said. Yet everywhere was the sound of life—birds, monkeys, a dog, a donkey—uninhibited by the imperial code of silence for those within calling distance of the palace.

He was paraded onto a terrace and forced to sit at a table. A bowl of rice arrived and he wolfed it down using his fingers as a scoop.

The sun kissed the mountaintops and hurled itself into the sky. He soaked in its warmth until it hid him under the shade of the bathhouse roof.

Bowing to the maid who had served him, he turned to face his guardians. The men wore black lamellar armor made from small rectangular plates of leather and iron. The plates had been laced into horizontal rows and reinforced with tortoise shells. One guardian held a full-length hook shield with a sword while the other brandished a straight shield and crossbow.

The heftier of the two stepped forward with sword drawn.

"I am Ban Chao, general to the heirs of Liu Bang, founder of the eternal kingdom where the true sun rises. The true emperor sees all, hears all, knows all. Today you will face judgment which is true and right. Walk."

Ardeshir counted one hundred and twenty steps to the edge of the judgment hall. The sun was high overhead as he stepped into the sacred space of truth. A golden throne inlaid with ivory and emeralds occupied a small dais. Chrysanthemums surrounded the dais. The earthy herbal aroma hovered all around the space.

"Kneel and bare your neck," the general ordered.

Ardeshir adjusted his silk robe and knelt without a word. His heart, however, bubbled up prayer after prayer to his own Lord. He bent low with his palms to the floor and waited.

The slightest of shadows passed along the periphery of his vision so he shut his eyes and prayed harder.

"Do not move!" General Ban Chao ordered. "The emperor demands two truths from you. What shall they be?"

Ardeshir turned his hands palm upward for permission to speak.

"Speak!"

He swallowed. "The Creator of heaven and earth has moved the finest of the seen and unseen worlds to establish his truth and beauty in the home of the Han ruler."

Ardeshir slowed his breathing and turned his palms downward as he waited. Silence reined, apart from the trumpeter swans' repeated calls back at the pond.

When enough time had elapsed for the hearer to weigh his truth, Ardeshir once again turned his palms upward for permission to speak.

"Speak!" the general commanded.

"The wisdom of a ruler multiplies with the wisdom of his advisors," Ardeshir said, "especially if his advisors know that the Way is the way."

Once again he rested his palms on the floor. Moisture coated them and he fought for internal stillness.

The cool breeze alerted him that evening had arrived—and he was still alive. He peeked through his lashes without daring to move anything else. The place appeared to be empty.

"You may move now," a feminine voice whispered.

He raised his head and slowly worked to stretch out each muscle. He got to his feet and saw the source of the voice: it was the princess, supported on each side by a guardian who appeared carved in stone. A single torch flickered from a stand behind them.

The princess slid forward effortlessly, the breeze seeming like an extension of her persona. Although the shadows hid the exquisite beauty he had witnessed at the pond, her silhouetted form was accompanied by the scent of jasmine.

"The Discerner of Truth likes your two truths," the princess said. "He has gone to ponder them. At least they have won you another sunset and sunrise. You are now assigned to be my teacher so I may understand the importance of truth."

Ardeshir bowed. "As you wish, my princess. When your heart is prepared to hear the true truth, my tongue will be prepared to share it."

The princess laughed and her laughter mimicked the tinkle of the chimes at the temple. "True truth? Is it not enough that there is any truth? What truth can a foreigner bring into the house of all truth?" She snaked toward him and ran her fingers through his hair. "The gods ordained that you should save me. What I want to know is how you came to be so close that you could save me in the first place. Did you observe me, desire me, hope to steal me away?"

He stood in place, as still as the guardians.

"That truth will be debated until the sun rises again." She backed away slowly. "The foreigner broke the emperor's edict that no one should touch his daughter, but how would a foreigner know this edict? And if we don't know the edict, are we still responsible for keeping it, even if it comes from the emperor?"

She walked to a shelf near General Ban Chao and picked up a small fruit. She rolled it across the floor toward Ardeshir. It stopped three strides short.

"Of course, there is another question under consideration," she continued. "Has the foreigner foiled the will and desires of the gods by saving the emperor's daughter or has he fulfilled a greater plan purposed by gods he may know of? As long as you see the sun rise, you will have something to teach me."

She sat in a chair and the two guardians hoisted it to shoulder-level. She didn't look back as the trio disappeared into the darkness.

A gust of wind blew out the torch and the night belonged to the frogs, the crickets, and the distant call of a leopard.

Ardeshir waited for moonlight and then carefully stepped along the pathway toward what he hoped was his room. The Way might be the way, but would he see another sunset?

Two

Ardeshir leaned against the bamboo balustrade as a hundred peasants below pounded tree bark, hemp, and linen into usable writing material. His shadow cast a soothing reminder that for seven sunrises and six sunsets he continued to live, eat, sleep, and teach. His sole pupil moved with grace. The yellow chrysanthemum rested comfortably in its black nest on the side of her head.

"For our lessons," the princess said with a delicate wave of her hand toward the workers, "truth must be captured in the mind, the soul, and the heart of nature." She shuffled across the small bridge over the koi pond. "Emperor Qin Shihuangdi burned all records of previous knowledge until his entire family was destroyed by our beloved founder. We are the rediscoverers, the rebuilders, the reorganizers of all that was lost and all that will be."

It certainly seemed that the emperor's industriousness and zeal for truth might accomplish such a thing.

"Our people would value such materials to record their writings and poetry," Ardeshir said.

With a coy smile, the princess raised her face toward the sun, spread her arms, and spun slowly in place. "We are in the world and the world is in us. So it was and so it will be."

To whom did this flower of a woman compare? Certainly not his mother. Daphne had been a queen among women, passionate in her love for her husband and children, zealous in her commitment to a cause, and quick in mind and tongue when challenged—yet gentle enough to break a boy's will with a whisper.

A fever had taken her shortly after the birth of her third son and a day after his own oath of manhood. The pang of loss bubbled below the surface.

The princess was also not like his adopted sister, Yas, who had become a ferocious warrior in her own right. Yas fought alongside the cataphract initiates, charging at full tilt on her black Friesian war horse while bareback. The beast's powerful sloping shoulders, muscular body, and long, thick mane and silky tail blended with Yas's own hair, streaming from under her helmet as she rode. She had been an intimidating force to grow up with.

Neither was the princess like his father's sister, Laleh. As queen of the Parthians, Laleh was a confident, suspicious, calculating, and entitled monarch used to having her way in a world of men. If Laleh had been able to persuade his father, Ardeshir would have been raised by the Magi to be the next King of Kings for the Persian throne. She would have smothered him, controlled him, protected him, elevated him, and pampered him until the world bowed at his feet.

The Magi were the kingmakers, royal advisors, and protectors of the Persian throne. Power rose and waned at their will. But they had no power in the emperor's garden.

As for this young woman, it didn't seem right to call her princess forever.

"What is your name?" he inquired.

The princess stopped midstride, pirouetting in place with arms spread wide again. "Such impudence to seek such an intimate truth. Do the commoners in your world seek such things from their royal overlords? Is it not enough to know I am the daughter of the Han emperor, the princess of the palace?"

"It is enough that you know who you are," he said. "Your name is the seed of your soul."

The princess crouched and snatched up a flower, breathing in its fragrance. "And is this name of yours the seed of your soul? Does it ask you why you live in such an insignificant body? Does it plague your dreams about who you might become in the shadow of your father?" She dropped the flower and crushed it underfoot. "Does the seed of your soul determine who you can marry? Does it crush you with boundaries and limits? Does it make you feel mindless?"

"Not all of those things."

Her lips puckered and her eyebrows furrowed. "Some thoughts seem like wisdom but are food for fish. Which is this saying of yours? Is it wisdom for the minds of the gods or waste for the stomach of fish?"

"You decide!"

"How can I know?"

"Such is today's lesson."

He left her in an orchard of peach trees, caressing the blossoms and weighing the path of wisdom aloud. She was like no woman he had met before.

Ardeshir sheltered in the guest quarters where all foreigners were sequestered for the length of their stay. Thin mahogany boards, loosely spaced, provided for the free flow of air in the room, which was little more than four strides by four strides. A thin feathered mattress kept him away from the insects and rodents scurrying by.

Ardeshir took every opportunity to find his peace elsewhere.

As the evening shadows lengthened, he perched on a peach tree and watched the gardener below. From this vantage, it was clear that the luxurious spread around him had been designed for reflection and escape from a world fixated on something other than peace. The landscape drew harmony between humanity and the natural world. Ponds, rock structures, sculptured trees, hedges, and flowerbeds flowed among halls, pavilions, and winding paths. The spot of his perch marked the edge of massive orchards and parks for hunting game.

The gardener glanced up nervously at the snarl of a leopard, and a moment later the young man joined him in the tree. His galloping Mandarin left Ardeshir feeling helpless.

Finally, the youth slowed his efforts at communication. "Leopard hungry. No feeding. Climb tree. Eat you. Go now."

The clarified message stimulated him to follow the gardener down the tree and along a winding path through hedges until he reached a shack, the roof of which could be reached by the branch of a plum tree. The youth lit the wick of a clay lamp from the firepit out front and moved inside where members of his family were laughing.

An elderly man with a white beard pointed to a small carpet beside himself. Ardeshir sat.

The young gardener nodded toward the old man. "Name. Zhao Chu. Father. My name. Liu."

"Ardeshir ben Nabonidus," Ardeshir introduced himself.

"You Shir. Prince Shir," Zhao Chu declared.

The others nodded and then focused on the food set before them. Liu named each item slowly in Mandarin. "Rice. Taro. Pear. Bamboo. Chestnut. Bean. Jerky from Peacock." He then handed Ardeshir a glistening porcelain cup with a blue dragon on it. "Your cup. Your home."

Ardeshir mumbled his memorized family prayer of gratitude to the Almighty and watched his host. Through hand gestures and short verbal prompts, he pointed out the food of interest and consumed his share.

Afterward Liu invited him to stay on a spare reed mat. Ardeshir slept sparingly as the moon painted the garden maze. The jasmine-tainted breeze caressed his face and an image of the princess filled his dreams.

Shortly after the moon slid from view, before the sun offered its first fingers of dawn, a gong rang over and over.

Liu tapped him and crawled to the doorway. "General hunt us," he said.

"What do you mean?" Ardeshir asked.

"General hunt us. Uses leopard. We hide. Come."

Ardeshir's heart thumped like a drum as he gasped for air. As he crouched outside the door, the surrounding pathways took on more distinctive shades of black. Liu faded into the night, leaving Ardeshir behind. His legs shook like leaves.

A final gong echoed through the chill air and the hair on his neck stood on end.

He heard footsteps thud on the bridge over the koi pond. The faintest swish of a branch drifted across the water. The snarl of a leopard split the black.

The embers from the dying fire drew Ardeshir's attention. In a flash, he quickstepped toward the base of the plum tree and began to scale it. Moments later, he slid onto the roof, feeling it bow slightly under his weight. He stiffened and held his breath.

The rattle of metal against wood on a nearby path broke the symphony of frogs and crickets. The brush around the clearing erupted and feet pounded on the hard-packed earth.

"Hunt!" someone roared with a guttural laugh. "Claws, Hunt!"

A human scream pierced the night a few minutes later. It was a sound Ardeshir hoped to never hear again.

Walking through the gardens the next day disturbed his stomach and left him running for his chamber pot. On the second day after the horrifying encounter, Ardeshir met Liu in an alcove burrowed into the wall of soil behind his modest home. The gardener was mixing powders.

"Should been me," Liu murmured in his stumbling Mandarin. Ardeshir tried to thank him for the meal with his family. "I the one with smell of foreigner. My sister serve princess."

"Your sister?"

It turned out that Liu's sister had been taken by the leopard in the general's hunt. Today Liu went about his work with great focus, offering little comment.

"What do you mean, 'the smell of the foreigner'?" Ardeshir pressed. "Are you saying you should have been eaten by the leopard because you invited me to your house?"

"Best you teach princess and best Liu garden. No come to my family. Leopard smell you."

Liu continued to work with the powders, refusing to look up.

"What are you doing?" Ardeshir asked.

"Shhh! Make fire medicine for leopard. Uncle invent but burn face and hands and house so stand away."

"What's in it?"

"Yellow powder, saltpeter, herb. Uncle look for secret to long life for emperor. Mix many powders but this one burns hard."

"How will this take care of the leopard?"

"We put in pile and sprinkle small line. We put lamp to line and whoosh. It blow leopard to pieces."

Ardeshir raised an eyebrow. "Aren't you afraid of hurting yourself?"

"Better destroy leopard for hope of many. Family must be protected."

"Does anyone know about this fire medicine?"

"No. Family secret. Come. I show you how to mix."

Watching the gardener carefully measure and mix the saltpeter, herbs, and yellow powder drew Ardeshir in, almost like a whirlpool sucking on his soul. What hidden powers lay in the mind and hands of this lowly gardener?

The two waited until late afternoon when the general was meant to be asleep. As the hours passed, they prepared for his midnight walk through the gardens.

At the appointed time, they crept to the farthest point in the garden from the palace. Liu carefully unfolded the cloth that held the powdered treasure. He sprinkled it around a small shed, set a small piece of twisted vine in the middle, and unwound it.

"Behind rock," Lui instructed, urging Ardeshir to lower his head.

The explosion was dramatic as a small shack twenty strides away was blown into the sky. They both dove for the ground and from that position lay smiling at each other. The general and the leopard had better watch out.

Life continued on as it had, except for the nights. Ardeshir set a shelf in front of the privacy curtain that served as the entrance to his room. Golden dragons were sewn into the rich blue cloth and during the day the sun passed through them to form intricate works of art. At night, however, these pets of the emperor were said to come alive and slither around the room. The branches scratching at the roof resembled the scrabbling of claws.

Sleep proved elusive. His pursuit of truth and pithy sayings proved grueling over the next week, considering the energy lull that followed.

He came across three men who sat under a red sandalwood tree at the edge of the pond, carving pieces of wood. They seemed so focused and peaceful that he worked hard to imitate them utilizing his own small knife. Their intricate animals and figurines were produced from camphorwood, cedar, gingko, mahogany, and longan wood. The red sandalwood also sacrificed a few of its branches in the process.

The effort was futile, though. Ardeshir's best work resembled the clumsy attempts of a child and the half-dozen unfinished projects he left around his room demonstrated that the art was beyond him.

After sitting for two hours beside the three carvers, Ardeshir held up his latest feeble attempt at carving a piece of mahogany.

The elder carver stroked his long white beard, took the carving, and ran his hands over it.

"The life of the wood is in the mind and hand of the creator," the elder said. "What do you see in this wood?"

Ardeshir smiled. "I see a dead koi rolled up into a sushi ball."

The man frowned. "Your problem is not your hand, but your mind. Take this back and imagine something beautiful."

Ardeshir accepted the wood and looked at it with renewed interest. "Before I try this again, how deep is this pond in the center?"

The second carver scooped up a rock and threw it. "Too deep."

The third carver chuckled. "My grandfather make pond when emperor plan garden. Pond is three man deep. No swim for people. Only fish."

"How did they get the water here?" Ardeshir asked. "It seems fresh."

"Good mind, my grandfather," the carver said. "Water by palace near den for lions. He make tunnel to feed pond. Hide it very carefully so no one find it."

The next afternoon, he grew so frustrated by his poor efforts that he threw his deformed chunk of mahogany into the koi pond. As it sank out of sight, the image of the princess's bone flute popped into his mind. In that moment, he formed a strategy to regain favor from the princess who had lately been ignoring him.

He waded into the pond while the three carvers watched him. The water was icy enough to take his breath away. But he'd survived it before while rescuing the princess...

If he recalled correctly, the bone flute would be near the deepest part of the pond.

The three carvers got to their feet as he bobbed up from his first dive. And on his fifth dive, they were still there.

After the twelfth dive, they helped pull him out at the shoreline.

This was going to be harder than it looked.

By his third day and thirty-second dive, it seemed he had run his hand through every inch of fish waste and muck at the bottom of the pond without success. His dives were drawing a larger crowd with each passing attempt and he was past embarrassment at dragging himself from the pond in his wet loincloth. The shock on the observers' faces, the discomfiture on others, only seemed to make the event more memorable compared to the everyday routine of these people's daily lives.

"Why do they think I'm doing this?" he asked the elder carver after his final dive on the third day.

"Some say you get mosquito infection, go crazy in the head. Some say you break rule of no swim deliberately so general feed you to leopard. Some say you lose something but forget where you put it. Some say you lose mind and forget where you lost it."

All three carvers were chuckling now.

On his fourth day, Ardeshir changed his strategy. He waited until noon when the sun shone directly over the pool, then disrobed at the water's edge. He absorbed the indrawn breaths of new spectators and swam to the middle of the pond. Inhaling deeply, he filled his lungs and floated facedown, searching the bottom for any sign of discoloration. The koi nibbled on his arms and legs but he floated motionless.

As he was about to surface for a breath, a faint line in the dark bottom caught the light. Taking note of the location, he slowly raised his head and gasped for air. When he had quieted his lungs, he breathed deeply over and over and then dove.

It took three more attempts, but on that third try he held up the bone flute triumphantly. The crowd on the shoreline, now numbering over fifty, clapped.

Within moments, four guardians rushed from the palace. By the time he reached shore, they were waiting for him. The first one pulled his wrist behind his back while the second snatched the flute.

"No noise near palace," a third guardian said. "You cause disturbance. No cheer for you."

The fourth man waved the crowd away.

Ardeshir was standing cold, wet, and bound when the general appeared.

"Troublemaker making trouble again?" the general asked. "No swim in the emperor's pond. No noise in the emperor's garden. No indecent exposure in the emperor's world." He swatted Ardeshir three times across the back and legs with his bamboo rod. "Go get dressed. We find punishment to make you respect the emperor."

Three

The punishment was isolation for two weeks in a cold underground storage cellar. Three guardians alternated shifts, repeating to him the rules of the kingdom over and over and over. The second guardian had a high-pitched tone that irritated Ardeshir's eardrums. Having no light or silence grated on his nerves and he broke down shouting several times, only to be beaten back into silence with a bamboo rod. Why had he come to this barbaric place?

The memory of his gladiator father presiding over their farm for orphans and widows in Susa grew dim. That farm was a place where people could get a new start. His mother had been a former priestess for Artemis, the goddess of healing in Ephesus, before she had escaped and followed Yeshua. His dad had been the emperor's champion in the arena and won his freedom by notching enough kills. Nabonidus had started a church in the home he'd purchased with his winnings.

However, a riot by those who opposed the new faith movement had forced them all to flee for their lives. He'd heard the stories growing up, but that all seemed so distant now.

Ardeshir had come on this journey to win the favor of the Han emperor for Persian trade. It had been a fruitless effort for almost two years, but then he had saved the princess from drowning.

Trying to retrieve her flute had clearly been an act of lunacy.

After what seemed an eternity, Ardeshir was released at night, dragged through dark trails, and dumped like a pile of fishing net at the entrance to his dwelling.

In the morning, Liu appeared and pulled him inside where for the next week he coaxed him back to strength. Every time Ardeshir woke up screaming, it was Liu who calmed him. When he gagged on his food, it was Liu who altered his diet and kept him nourished.

The first day Ardeshir stepped out onto his balcony to absorb sunlight, he heard the clear tones of the bone flute playing from the palace.

Liu stepped up beside him as they surveyed the pond together. "General take credit for getting flute. No one say different. You not tell princess what happened."

Ardeshir shook his head as if shaking off the water from the pond. "No! No, no, no. She deserves to know. I nearly died trying to get her precious little flute. The general has no right."

Liu skirted in front of him and bowed low and on the ground. "General have right. General is general. He is emperor's unicorn."

"I noticed the general has a unicorn patch on his robe and one of the guardians has a lion," noted Ardeshir. "What does this mean?"

"Unicorn is highest position for military man. You know who people are by patch on their robe. No confusion in kingdom. Everyone know who they are."

Carrying his father's blood in his veins and his mother's soul in his body didn't seem to matter in this empire. No one knew who these outsiders were that Ardeshir represented. If the situation didn't improve soon, he would have to go home and give up this pointless mission.

Then who would he be?

Liu sprang to his feet like a playful dog. "Come. You come with Liu. We see hunting park. Not think of princess. Come!"

Ardeshir grudgingly set his feet on the path Liu chose. Breathing heavily, he halted as the climb around the back of the palace grew steeper. In the two years since he'd arrived in the land of the Han, taking refuge in the emperor's garden, he'd never dared to take this path. He'd once seen the black leopard lying on a tree limb hanging over it.

"Come!" Liu urged, waving his hand in urgency. "Breathe. Step. Breathe. Step."

The sun halted directly overhead to peer down on them. There was no place to hide from its rays.

He was panting hard by the time Liu stopped next to a tall stone wall. The gardener pointed toward a mahogany tree whose branches hung over the wall.

"Climb and see!" Liu said. "Park for wild things."

The process of climbing after Liu was slow and painful. The younger man was agile and knew the tree well. But by stepping where Liu stepped, he scaled the tree and slid along it until he could perch on the top of the wall.

From their roost, Liu handed over a small leather sack of fruit pieces and Ardeshir slurped them down. The effort was refreshing.

By tracing the top of the wall, he could see that the hunting park extended far into the forest. He spotted a new body of water, three times the size of the koi pond near the palace. This one was surrounded by the barren ground that sprawled just beyond the wall.

Movement near a copse of trees caught his attention.

"Elephant come," Liu said. "Hungry for lichi nut."

The man pulled a second leather pouch from his robe and grabbed a handful of sun-dried fruit. The treats were bright red with a leathery outer shell. The white grape-like flesh inside had turned to a raisin-like texture.

As the elephant neared, its ears flared like giant fans that moved slowly back and forth. Ardeshir's stomach churned at the beast's mammoth size.

Liu put out a hand with the treats. "Elephant not know you. Ears flap mean not happy. We leave treat and come back."

Liu laid the treats carefully on top of the wall and backed away toward the tree they'd used to climb onto it. As he did, the elephant trumpeted and charged.

Ardeshir almost collapsed in terror as the giant bore down on them.

Liu grabbed his elbow and tugged hard. "Come!"

He didn't have to hear the command twice. As they skittered along the branch on their way back to the ground, the elephant wrapped its trunk around its end and began to shake. It seemed like a miracle when the two men made it safely down.

Liu took one look at his friend's face and then rolled on the ground in a belly laugh. "You should see your eyes," he choked out. "Big like elephant's."

Moments later, a palace guardian with an extra-long javelin raced up the path.

"Did you bother animals?" the guardian demanded. "Did you see any peoples?"

Liu stood straight-faced. "We hear elephant. Maybe he trying to be rooster. Make noise."

The guardian raced past them.

Liu chuckled all the way back.

The princess sat cross-legged on a small dais in a patch of sunlight, hands folded, face lifted. An arc of circular baskets formed a boundary around her. Peasants covered in peaked straw hats paraded by, depositing offerings of wheat, rice, foxtail, millet, beans, chestnuts, pears, peaches, melons, mustard greens, and taro.

Ardeshir perched on a garden wall and watched the baskets, but most of all he paid attention to his sole pupil. This routine was familiar now. The princess had to count to one thousand while the peasants gave their offerings. Too much sun was said to spoil the delicate texture of her features and flawless skin.

The time for instruction would come after her bath and massage, when she was relaxed enough to contemplate the truths Ardeshir would offer.

General Ban Chao stood at the entrance to the palace and ripped off chunks of naan to each peasant who had given their gift. The general had discovered this unusual type of bread during a military campaign in the west and had captured a skilled baker to provide the flatbread as a show of generosity. But his visage was as cold and firm as granite.

The necessity of sitting cross-legged for an entire hour during his lessons with the princess got easier as the days passed and the posture became more natural. Between lessons, Ardeshir would venture outside to drink in the sounds of the birdlife, animals, and even insects. He used the time to prepare the lessons, including rich stories of his faith that would convey the thought-provoking nuggets of truth intended to stretch the young woman's mind.

In today's lesson, he was teaching about the unity of all peoples based on the story of a worldwide flood. Only eight had been saved!

But the story wasn't going over well.

"What foolishness is this?" the princess spouted. "Do you dare imply that a man like the general has no right to hunt the peasants with his leopard?"

Ardeshir winced. The general stood nearby, targeting his crossbow on a large orangutang that was clambering across the roof of the palace. Fortunately, the man didn't seem to have heard the princess's comment.

The princess tried again, a little louder. "Are you implying that the emperor and his family have no more standing in the world than a small-minded foreigner like yourself? That we are merely monkeys sporting about in the trees, unworthy of our pleasures and palaces?"

The general perked up this time.

"Dear one on whom the sky smiles," Ban Chao called to her. "I am happy to cut your teacher in strips for the leopard or chop him up in chunks for the koi. What is your pleasure?"

The princess jutted out her chin and smirked. "There! Finally, a man who respects me for who I am." She glared at Ardeshir. "What shall I do with my choice?"

What had he got himself into? Ardeshir's gaze turned to the general's toothy leer. It seemed no one had ever successfully wedged their way between the princess and the general, and Ardeshir wasn't about to change that now.

The general slowly raised his loaded crossbow. The point of the arrow appeared especially sharp as it glistened in the sun.

"Not the crossbow," the princess stated calmly as though choosing an outfit to wear. "And not the leopard. Too quick. How can I teach a teacher his place in my world?"

Being stretched above the koi pond with the whole compound watching felt humiliating. The experience had been designed with humiliation in mind. The sisal ropes tied around Ardeshir's wrists and his ankles burned as they chafed his skin. When the wind blew through the branches holding those ropes, pushing them even a few inches, it threatened to pull him apart.

At least the princess had consented to allow him a loincloth.

The lurch in his stomach at all this swaying and stretching launched him back to his boyhood when his father had taught him to ride at a gallop. Yas had been a natural, but the movement of the horse nauseated Ardeshir.

His aunt, the queen of the Parthians, had eyed him closely during one of his training sessions. At the end of his ride, she pronounced the obvious to his father: "If your son is going to rise through the ranks to even be considered for his role as King of Kings, I will have to see more courage, more joy, more passion in his ride. Weakness is not a virtue of our people."

His failure to thrive on a horse was a likely reason for having been assigned to this trade mission far from home.

At the high point of Ardeshir's fluctuating arc, he reached the height of three towering generals above the water. At the low point, it was perhaps less than one gardener. The koi swam nonchalantly back and forth until the princess busied herself with throwing bits of rice and other goodies to them.

"How happy are the fish who know how to respect the one who feeds them," she said. "How is it that everyone except one knows their place in our world?"

The peasants lined up along the edge of the pond, bowing and nodding as the princess stood against the railing of the small bridge. Several of them knelt with their faces to the ground and their hands spread out in front of them.

The princess scanned the group and then waved the general to her side. After a brief discussion, she pointed out Liu, one of the peasants with his face down. The general nodded toward another warrior who hurried to the gardener, yanked him to his feet, and marched him to the base of the bridge.

Liu bowed to the ground again.

"On your feet, peasant," the princess said. "I have chosen you to take the teacher's place so you can show him how to honor those over you. Would you like to honor the emperor's daughter?"

Liu rose to his feet, head still bowed but nodding vigorously.

The princess spoke loudly. "General, cut down the teacher."

"No!" Ardeshir yelled. "I will not allow another to take my punishment."

He continued to swing gently as the princess and general eyed him like a bird aloft.

He spoke loudly again. "The truth for today is that the innocent who are punished bring no honor to their masters."

Ardeshir closed his eyes, which may have been a mistake. His sudden spreadeagled plunge into the pond stung like no other sting he had felt before. He gasped, swallowing water, and fought to disentangle his arms and legs from the ropes which held him under.

Finally, relaxing, he rose and broke the surface, gagging, coughing, and gasping for air.

The general grinned from ear to ear, but the princess was nowhere in sight. Liu remained bowing at the base of the bridge. It seemed his friend was safe for now.

Four

Two weeks after his bellyflop into the koi pond, Ardeshir shivered in the shade of the balcony outside his room. The tight wrap around his wrist secured the fracture he'd sustained by getting caught in the twisting rope during his suspension over the water. The sense of emptiness inside continued to suck him dry. Not even Lui's offerings of rice and fruit tempted him to reach for nourishment.

Dreams of home crowded out his sleep, but they were no longer visions of joy and hope. Yas galloped past him on her Friesian warhorse, raising her javelin and laughing at his feeble efforts to hang on. Aunt Lelah wrapped her royal robes tighter and backed away as though he was a leper about to defile her. His father sat in a corner, head in his hands, sighing.

Then a flute sounded among the shadows. A finger of sunlight caressed his cheek. The faintest taint of jasmine tickled his nostrils. A cool wet cloth wiped his brow and a trail of liquid life crept through his beard, across his jaw, and down his neck. His heart pounded in his ears and his fists released.

"He live," Lui said. "He live."

Day after day, the flute continued to play as Lui dragged the reed mat into a corner of the balcony where the sun shone longer. The rice and fruit found favor in his belly, the throb in his wrist lessened, and his dreams embraced more hope.

"Do you know what I dreamed of last night?" Ardeshir asked one morning.

"What you dream?" Lui responded.

"That my sister came to visit me." He winced as he pushed himself up to sit against the railing. "She came, saw me, and smiled at me."

"Good sister!" Lui said. "Come! Today see princess play flute in boat."

The last thing he wanted was to watch that wretched princess play her flute. For all he cared, she could tip over that pitiful little craft and fall to the bottom of the pond with the koi. Saving her had been the worst decision of his life and he'd had nothing but trouble ever since. Had he gained any favor with his father? None at all. No one cared an iota about truth or anything else he thought or said.

He watched Lui scrub his soiled clothing nearby and lamented what a pitiful sight he must be in his filth. It would have been far better if he had sacrificed himself to the leopard so Liu hadn't lost a sister. What kind of a wretched place was this where generals could hunt peasants with impunity? What kind of an empire was this where the emperor's daughter could humiliate her teacher without a second thought?

He pushed away his food and started beating his fists against the sides of his head.

Lui displayed amazing strength and self-control as he seized Ardeshir's wrists and forced them to be limp.

"Still like the lotus," he chanted. "Soft like the breeze. Gentle like mother. Peaceful like babe."

The flute broke through again, playing a haunting melody—one that carried the words of an old psalm: "Be still and know that I am He. Be still and know that I am here. Be still."

His mother's face smiled down on him. Her soothing words cradled the psalm in her tongue.

"Sweet, sweet Ardeshir," she whispered. "Son of my heart. My twice-found son."

He knelt and rose to his feet with the help of Lui.

"It is time to live again, my friend," Ardeshir said. "Perhaps it's time for me to return home, even if I haven't found a way to bring honor to my father."

"The princess plays for your life," Lui said.

Ardeshir glanced toward the pond and then turned away. "She can play for the koi, for all I care. She has stolen the last ounce of dignity I had just to prove that she is someone. I no longer care who she is or who she wants to be."

"Maybe bath make you feel better."

It took a lot of baths before he finally felt better, although at least Lui's food filled him with strength. The flute music faded into the background noise of the garden, mixed with birdsong, workers tilling, donkeys braying, and a dog barking.

One morning he stopped Lui as the man swept his balcony. "How are you spending so much time with me? Won't the general feed you to the leopard if you don't get your gardening done?"

Lui smiled. "Princess choose me to show honor." He put his fist on his chest. "My life for your life. You die, I die. You live, I live."

Ardeshir had to shake his head at that one. None of what had happened made any sense to him. He had been trying to teach the ungrateful lotus blossom a little truth, yet she'd done her best to kill him. Well, to humiliate him first and *then* kill him. Women! Who could figure them out?

He expected that truth would haunt him all of life. For now, he would avoid the balcony and stop listening to that annoying flute.

On his first walk away from the koi pond and garden, Ardeshir stumbled upon a market he hadn't noticed in his earlier explorations. Rows of wooden stalls, neatly ordered under fluttering red canopies, occupied one side of the dirt path; from there, fruit vendors sold peaches, plums, melons, apricots, bayberries, jujubes, pears, and chestnuts. From the other side, under white canopies, vendors sold mustard greens, taro, bamboo shoots, beans, millet, rice, barley, calabash, wheat, and foxtail. At the far end stood vendors under brown canopies who sold chickens, fish, rabbits, pigs, dogs, donkeys, and various rodents and birds in cages. The cacophony was a tsunami of sensory overload after the enforced silence of the emperor's palace.

Apart from the separated rows of colored canopies, it reminded him much of the market stalls in Susa.

A pang of loneliness enveloped Ardeshir and the sights and sounds of this crowded place closed around his mind and spirit like a suffocating blanket. He fought to still his rapid breathing and push his way past the elbows, knees, and woven baskets of the customers.

He was still bent over gasping for air when someone tapped him on the shoulder.

"Not your day for the market, I see," a voice said. "Come to my shop for tea and rest a while so you can catch your breath."

Ardeshir allowed himself to be led by the elbow to a small shop near the entrance to the market. Here, small eateries formed a pattern much like petals around a flower. In the center of this square splashed a small fountain.

He noticed that the vendor was wiry and thin, with a long white goatee and peaked red cap with yellow tassels dangling from the peak. The man sported a brilliant blue wide-sleeved mianfu robe; the shirt underneath was covered with dragons and elongated lions. The hem of the robe was red and inlaid with stars, moons, and twisting vines.

"What is your name?" Ardeshir asked as he accepted the teacup and nested it in his palms to warm himself.

"Ah! The question you still have no answer for from the princess." The old man shuffled into a back room and returned with a plate of edibles. "You are Persian, so you need food we are only learning to eat. This is mutton jerky, dried in my own shop. This is yogurt which may have sat too long for your tastes."

The jerky was chewier and the yogurt sourer than the fare he had grown accustomed to in Susa, but he nodded in gratitude. No words were exchanged as the shopkeeper dealt with other customers.

When Ardeshir set his cup down, the vendor examined the tea leaves on the bottom. "I see that you shall have a visitor from Persia soon."

"You can see that in my tea leaves?" Ardeshir asked.

The vendor smiled. "No! One of my customers saw a caravan outside the city. He noticed there were Persians among the group and then took notice of you. I put the two together." He removed the cup and plate and laid a small cookie in its place before closing his eyes and folding his hands, palms together. "Your fortune is this: the desire of your heart is beyond you, but the dream of your soul is much closer than you imagine."

Ardeshir nodded. "Now that's a truth I should share with the princess."

"Save it for yourself." The old man smiled. "Behind you are three strangers posing as local Han farmers. They are spies of the Yayoi emperor, who rules over his 'islands of the sun.' We call his land Wa and their people Yamoto." He picked up a broom and swept the ground. "You must tell the princess that three Yamoto from Wa have come to pluck her heart. She will know what to do."

Ardeshir nodded in appreciation, then laid a coin on the table and strolled back toward his accommodation.

No sooner had he washed himself than a small chime sounded outside his door.

Upon opening it, he encountered Liu standing alongside a guardian of the palace. The soldier's vest was made from rhino skin and plated with shells and metal squares that had been sewn into place. His metal helmet covered his ears and hung down to protect his neck. A crossbow and javelin provided his weaponry and a metal shield hung over his shoulder.

"Health to the Persian speaker of truth," the guardian called. "A message from the emperor."

Ardeshir nodded.

"A caravan has arrived from Persia. One of the newcomers seeks an audience with you. The emperor wishes to employ your services to translate all that is needed."

"And I have news for the princess," Ardeshir replied. "Three Yamoto have come to pluck her heart."

The guardian raised his eyebrows and quick-stepped away.

Liu hung back, waiting patiently outside the door. "I will take you to the caravan when you are ready…"

Translating for the general demanded solid concentration. The big man rattled off his thoughts in Mandarin while jabbing Ardeshir with his elbow, trying to get his message across through physical stimulation. A corridor had been formed between a long row of Persian traders and hundreds of Han vendors. These caravansary traders were spreading out their wares upon rich Persian carpets.

The caravan chief rattled back answers in Farsi, just as quickly and with as much passion. Both men seemed to determine to speak over each other as they fought for a clear understanding of the negotiations and Ardeshir struggled to carry the translation.

He gathered that this caravan had been on the trail for three months, facing harsh weather, several ambushes from bandits, and poor service from ill-equipped caravansaries. There had been sicknesses and losses. They weren't about to return home without turning a profit.

The general flaunted the quality of silk available through the emperor's own craftsmen.

"This is the only place in the world where you can find these shimmering wonders designed by the wife of the Yellow Emperor, Huangdi," Ban Chao declared. "If any of your people are found smuggling silkworm eggs, cocoons, or mulberry seeds, they will be immediately cut into pieces and fed to our lions."

"We have no intention of feeding your lions," the caravan chief replied. "We did not come here for worms."

The chief went on to boast that they had started the journey with forty donkeys, sixty camels, forty armed horsemen, and twenty oxcarts. They had lost ten donkeys, five camels, and three oxcarts, plus two armed guards who had been killed in the ambushes. Thirty-seven traders had stayed with the journey to the end.

The general laughed at the chief's rendition. "I know you made a hefty profit off each trader. You probably promised the moon and gave them the cheapest accommodation, the simplest food, the least comfort and protection."

In his translation, Ardeshir tried to tone down these derogatory phrases to ease the tension.

The Persian cataphracts, with their heavily armored horses, stood with lances poised while the emperor's own guardians raised crossbows and javelins. One of the cataphracts at the far end of the line reined his charge around and cantered toward the bargainers—and only at the last minute did Ardeshir look up to see the smiling face of his sister, Yas.

The distraction earned him an extra sharp elbow from the general.

Ardeshir finished the negotiations and left the traders and craftsmen to their tasks. Yas seemed to have grown another six inches since he'd left home. Her plumed helmet defined her as the chief of the cataphract band.

He bowed to her and she struck him on the shoulder with the butt of her javelin, staggering him sideways.

The general stepped into the gap with his shield up and sword drawn.

"He's my brother," Yas said from her defensive stance. She turned to Ardeshir: "Tell him, you're my brother."

Ardeshir took his stance beside the general. "It is dishonorable to the emperor to attack someone in his kingdom who is greeting you as I have done. You must choose how you will restore honor to the emperor."

"You're my brother," she said. "I'm the captain of the cataphracts. We've come three months to see you."

Ardeshir bowed. "You must restore honor or the general will be forced to declare war on all of you."

Yas screwed up her face and shook her head. "Who are you? Tell the general I will do what is necessary to restore the honor for the emperor."

When the translation was complete, the general lowered his shield and sword and nodded his bald head. "Come!" he ordered in Mandarin.

Yas awaited the translation, then fell into step with her brother. Several others followed until they reached the bridge over the koi pond.

"Wait!"

The general marched stately toward a white-plastered hut where two guardians stood stiffly. At his nod, one of the guardians opened the door. The three Yamoto, stripped to their loincloths, were escorted out.

Ban Chao pointed at another guardian, who hurried to a nearby hut. From inside, he produced three shields, three swords, three armored vests, and a suit of battle gear. The Yamoto were ordered to dress for battle; they did, although their weapons were placed at the edge of the bridge.

"Translate for the Persian," the general ordered. "Whoever cross bridge alive will live. You kill Yamoto, then honor of Emperor is restored. They kill you, then honor of Emperor is restored and they go free." He passed on a similar message to the three Yamoto who understood perfectly what was at stake.

The general withdrew and yelled, "Cross bridge now!"

Five

The three Yamoto floating facedown in the koi pond appeared so peaceful compared to the trauma they had just experienced under the fury of the Persian cataphract. Yas stood at the center of the bridge as she turned to the general and bowed.

"The emperor's honor is restored," she announced in Farsi.

There was no need for translation.

"I could have used you a few times in the last months," Ardeshir said, joining her. "Remind me to never make you my enemy."

"What happened to your wrists?" Yas asked. "I can kill whoever did that to you."

"I am trying to learn how to do things right in this place." He pulled the sleeves of his robe over his exposed wrists. "I am not always successful."

"Why are you always trying to please people who really don't matter? Why do these people matter to you? They're not your family."

"I don't think of myself as pleasing people. I'm just trying to survive wherever I am and with whomever is around me."

"Your father wants you to return and to learn how to fight for your kingdom," she said. "These spies will only be replaced by better spies. Your father is getting older and the population grows restless for a successor."

As a school of koi pecked at the bloodied hand of one of the dead Yamoto, Lui launched a boat to drag the bodies out of the pond.

Ardeshir snagged the bloodied javelin from Yas and, using the blade, dragged a corpse closer to the shore.

"My mission here may not yet be over," he said. "Clearly, Father sent you to finish one part of it for me. How can I run a kingdom if I cannot establish a peace treaty and a trade mission with an ally?"

"Who is the girl watching you?" Yas asked.

"Which girl?" He scanned the crowd.

"Keep your eyes down," she muttered. "The high-class girl on the second floor sheltering behind a plant. She watches you closely."

Ardeshir dropped the javelin on the bridge deck. As he scooped it up, he glanced at the palace. Someone ducked back at the window.

"She is a former student of mine," he answered.

"Is she enough to keep you here?" His sister always had been straightforward in her speech.

"She's the emperor's daughter. She tried to have me killed."

Using the spear, Ardeshir guided one of the bodies toward Liu in the boat. The gardener tied a rope to the corpse's arm.

"I see she failed," Yas continued. "Would marrying her accomplish your mission and please your father?"

He thrust the shaft of the spear back into her hand and leaned against the railing. "You've killed three men since you arrived and restored the honor of the emperor. I have done nothing except dishonor his daughter over and over." He pulled the sash on his robe tighter. "When you speak of Father, you must address him as *our* father. We are a family."

"The only family resemblance about us is the shade of our skin, neither dark as dusk nor light as dawn. You are the firstborn even if they ignore my adoption and dub me the eldest. I will always be a warrior on a horse and you will be a prince on a throne."

Yas caught his attention.

"There's one more thing I have to tell you," she added. "Your two brothers and your sister died in a plague last year. Your father has no one but you to depend on now."

This revelation shook Ardeshir to his core. How was he going to carry the honor of his father, his family, and his nation?

But he had no time to ponder these questions.

The general intercepted the cataphracts as they descended off the bridge.

"The emperor will honor you for restoring his honor and securing his life," said Ban Chao. "There will be a banquet tonight once the trading is finished. We must complete our business and make our people happy."

Yas nodded and followed the straight-backed general toward the throng milling about the trade goods spread out in the distance. Lui paddled the boat, dragging all three bodies back to the shore where others had stretched out three hemp bags for burial cloths.

The Yamoto would not end up as fish food. Even defeated enemies had a dignity to be preserved.

A palace guardian and a maiden waited for Ardeshir at the entrance to his room. The guardian nodded faintly and the young girl bowed with her face to the ground; her hands held out a piece of hemp paper slightly larger than her hands.

Ardeshir snatched up the paper and read the Mandarin script. The characters were neatly fashioned and the lines precise. The message was simple: *"Come!"*

"Wait!" he said to her. "I need to wash and change."

Would the princess understand his need for presentability or would she chafe under the passing sun and consider a new form of torture for him to endure? What was wrong with this girl?

She better not humiliate me in front of my sister, he thought.

Yas had proved what she was capable of if honor was at stake. He shuddered as images of the short battle on the bridge replayed in his mind.

He hurried through his rituals and stepped behind the guardian to the palace's rear entrance. At the arched doorway, another maiden waited with another paper. Another clear message in the same script. *"Follow!"*

The maiden and another palace guardian marched through a maze of hedges and around rows of flowers and small fountains until they reached the upper heights of the palace grounds. A gazebo, neatly camouflaged behind hanging vines, blended in with the trees. The princess paced inside the hidden alcove.

"What took you long?" she erupted in crude Persian. "I wait."

He dropped to his knees, facedown, and placed his palms against the earth. When sufficient time had passed, he turned them up for permission to speak.

"Oh, get to your feet," she said in flawless Mandarin again. "Why must you plague me with questions that grow in my mind? Now you bring your sister as a warrior to kill. Who are you people and why do you come?"

He rose to his feet and lowered his eyes, waiting.

She stepped out from the gazebo and stomped up to him, looking up into his face. "Speak truth to me. You come peaceful as a lotus, chanting poetry and song. You observe me like a man and save me from the water. Then you humiliate my honor." She spun in place. "Tell me: who are you when you are as still as the willow, as soft as the flute, as pure as the moonlight? Why have you come to haunt me?"

He dared to register the desperation in her eye and exasperation in her voice. "Do you wish the truth from my lips or my heart?" he asked.

She glared as she cocked her head and forced his eyes to stay on her face. "So it is so. I almost fed my maiden to the leopard because I swore her to tell me the truth about you. She has been watching you for the length of two full moons and swore to me on her life that your heart longed for me as a man for a woman."

Ardeshir dropped to his knees but maintained his gaze. "Forgive me," he said. "A man cannot always control his heart, eyes, or tongue."

"What does this mean? Forgive me."

He sat back on his haunches, grasping for the right words. "To forgive means to count something as never having happened." He shook his head. "Even though something bad has happened, you don't hold it against the other person." He raised his hands in a gesture of humility. "I am asking you to choose to ignore any look, word, action, or thought your maiden saw which made her feel that my heart to you was only that of a man for a woman."

"So you don't feel toward me like a man for a woman? I will have to feed my maiden to the leopard after all."

"No!" He stepped toward her and two of the guardians standing below the gazebo raised their crossbows and set their stance to shoot. He dropped to his knees again. "My heart wants what my heart can't have. Your maiden has seen what your maiden has seen. She has spoken her truth and does not deserve to die."

The princess stepped down onto the grass again and came to him. She raised her palm as if to slap him then lowered her hand.

"Truth is meant to calm the soul, clear the mind, bring peace to the heart," she said. "Nothing is clear, calm, or peaceful when you speak. I could give my heart to a man of truth, but I cannot be near a man who does not know how to speak the truth that brings life."

Ardeshir sank back to sit on his heels. "Princess, more than anything I would love to be that man of truth. But the leopard has eaten my courage, the koi have stolen my strength, and the birds have taken my truth for their nests."

The princess pulled a matching piece of hemp paper from a pocket in her robe. She handed it to him.

"When you find the courage of your sister, send me this message," she said. "I wanted to take you to the banquet to see the honor given to a pure soul, but I cannot be seen with you like this. Go back to your room."

He sat cross-legged, unwashed, and unmoving for two days. As the sun crested the roof of the palace, he opened his hand and released the hemp paper which the princess had given him. He stared at it past noon. His cracked lips, gungy mouth, dry tongue, and short quick breaths gave him pause to self-examine.

The paper unfolded easily, and upon it were four neatly scripted words. A name and an order.

"Lu Hou. Come soon."

The princess had shared her secret, the seed of her soul. Her name. Despite his cowardice, she had heard beyond the truth he was able to stutter. She had invited him to embrace both courage and strength.

He washed quickly and then looked across the pond toward the palace, but there was no princess in sight. The loud clash of gongs and sweet trills of flutes and mouth organs betrayed the reality that the banquets honoring the Persian delegation continued each night. The clash of weaponry from the field on the other side of the palace demonstrated that the soldiers from both armies were demonstrating their prowess. Yas was no doubt at the very center of it all, and the princess would likely be wondering how he could be so poorly suited for manhood when his sister was so gifted.

He clutched the message in his grip, his thoughts turning to his finest set of clothing. This sparked a surge of confidence and hope.

He craned his neck out his door and motioned for a servant girl. "Water!" he called in Mandarin.

A bowl of cool, clear water was soon laid at his door. He slid it indoors, washed himself thoroughly, chose his finest robes, and slid out into the evening air.

Despite the weakness in his legs from extended periods of disuse, he pushed hard across the bridge at the koi pond and continued along the path between the garden's hedges.

Liu waved him down as he rounded the last bend toward the back door of the palace. The gardener then bowed and waited until Ardeshir pulled him to his feet.

"Come, my friend," said Ardeshir. "We are almost brothers. There is no need to humble yourself in such a way."

Liu glanced toward the palace. "It is the way of our people. Every person must know their place so the empire and world will work in harmony. You look like you have hope in your eyes."

"Yes!" Ardeshir held out his folded paper. "The princess has invited me to come to her."

Liu stepped back, palms to his cheeks. "May the leopard eat all my children if I withhold the truth I must speak in the shadow of the emperor."

Ardeshir stepped forward onto Liu's shadow. "What truth is so strong to require such an oath?"

Liu took another step away, freeing his shadow. "The princess only yesterday had her day of recognition for womanhood. The rulers from all over the empire have sent their sons to compete for her hand so they can have their houses linked to the house of the emperor. She has been secluded for seven days now, unable to speak to anyone until a suitable choice is agreed on."

The lurch in his stomach and dizziness in his mind made Ardeshir stumble to a bamboo stool. He sank down on it and rested his head on his fist.

What had he done? The princess had given him the chance to declare himself and he had faltered. She had invited him to find his courage and come soon, but instead he had withdrawn in self-condemnation, tormenting himself with the inadequacy of who he was compared with his sister.

If the leopard had been nearby, he would have thrown himself into the path of those waiting jaws. If the elephant had reached out to grab him, he would have let it happen.

At that moment, he knew all was lost. His humiliation was complete. He would return to face his father as a failure.

Six

A month into his journey away from the emperor's palace, Ardeshir rested on a rocky outcropping which offered a sight of the highest peaks in the world. The cataphracts grew edgy as they set up camp above a long river valley.

Yas dismounted and came to stand beside him, admiring the panoramic view.

"Last chance!" she said. "Once we push through this part of the Silk Road, we won't encounter any other caravans until after winter. The tribes through here grow rich off their ambushes on poorly defended traders. No matter how big we seem to them, they always have to try."

"Are you sure Father wants me home?" Ardeshir asked. "I failed him on this trade mission. In one month among the Han, you gained more honor than I gained in two years."

Yas plunked down beside him. "You call what I had to eat at those banquets an honor?"

"I never did ask what they served you. I just assumed it was the normal rice and fruits."

She shook her head and grimaced. "I think they tested me as much with the food as with the fighting." She ran her fingers through her hair. "I put so many strange things in my mouth. They killed a dog in front of me and roasted it. They brought a monkey and had us eat its brain while it lived. We ate mice and piglets and sea cucumbers and a shark's fin and snake and even donkey."

"You ate a donkey?"

"They said that eating donkey here is like eating dragon in the beyond."

"I would have stood and told them about the life beyond where Yeshua has made us to live," Ardeshir said.

Yas stood and brushed off her robe. "If only I had learned like you. Next time I will beg them to send you." She moved to her horse and began searching through her pack.

"Remember, I'm the one who failed," he said. "The emperor probably wouldn't ask me to a banquet even if I did return."

Yas threw a gourd of cheap wine to him. "Drink something to drown your foolishness. The only one you failed is yourself, for not declaring yourself to the emperor's daughter. The two of us could have taken on any pair of those weak-kneed suitors who showed up to claim her. You've been so distracted on this trip that the ambushers could come and go and you probably wouldn't even notice."

"You need to teach me to fight before I get home. I can't shame Father twice. He was a gladiator. Yet my only weapon is my tongue."

Yas chuckled. "That, my brother, was as lame as one of your poems. The emperor's land has wilted your tongue to become as soft as a lotus blossom. I see how you despise your horse and seek every opportunity to get off and stretch."

"You're right," Ardeshir admitted. "I'm soft, weak, and a source of shame to my family."

Yas threw a knife between his feet and laughed again as he jumped. "Listen! The general negotiated a deal for one thousand of our Persian horses. I told him that you personally would lead those horses back to him. Our wagons are loaded with silk, jade, and many other treasures based on my word and your commitment... so you had better start paying attention to the challenges of this road or you will die out here."

He grabbed the knife and stepped toward Yas. The sky and ground suddenly changed orientation and he gasped for breath.

"I think I have more to teach you than I imagined," she said.

He was still gasping as he lay on the ground, resting on his back.

Yas walked back toward the men who respected her leadership and trusted her skills in the ambushes ahead.

Maybe it would have been better to take my chances with the princess and the general, he reflected.

The next morning, a small band of riders galloped toward the camp.

"Brace yourself," Yas yelled to the caravan.

The lead rider was waving a red banner similar to the one which had flown over the emperor's palace.

"Wait!"

The approaching force slowed to a trot and then walked as they came nearer. Yas went out ahead of the caravan to meet them with a small group of her own captains.

The lead rider handed her a small bag, then reined in his horse, turned, and galloped off to a waiting point about a mile from the Persians. What were they waiting for?

Yas held the bag out to Ardeshir as she turned away from the retreating riders.

"No attack," she said to him. "The emperor's guardians had a delivery for you. Something from the princess. Are you sure you don't want to go back with them?"

Ardeshir stepped away from the group to obtain a moment of privacy and opened the cloth bag. Inside were two pieces of hemp paper, each one with a neatly handwritten note. He dumped them onto his palm.

The messages were clear. The first contained one word: *"Coward."* The second included a short phrase: *"Return what you have stolen."*

His heart beat faster as he pushed the notes into the pocket of his robe. Coward? Thief? If he'd ever harbored fantasies of a life with the princess, that fantasy died.

No one else would ever see the notes. No way could he ever return to deliver the horses Yas had promised. The final tie had been severed.

He signaled to the guardians to return without him.

The first attack came a week later as the caravan forded a river upon rafts of logs they had cut and fastened together. There was no warning. Half of the people had already crossed and the other half were loading when the ambush occurred. The attackers struck from a point behind where Yas and Ardeshir rode side by side with a dozen other cataphracts and a small band of archers.

Suddenly, a river of arrows pierced horses, traders, camels, and any other valuable asset. Yas pivoted to face the attack and her comrades joined her in raising their shields.

Across the river, another band of marauders charged down out of the hills to stimulate chaos among the group unloading and attempting to organize themselves. The cataphracts who had gone ahead tried to establish a protective perimeter while a band of archers used the crossbows they'd secured from the Han general to return a deadly assault.

Three of the archers near Yas fell under the assault and she hurled herself onto one of the crossbows lying abandoned. She projected her vengeance on the lead ambushers rushing down the hill, their swords swinging.

"Pick up a bow," she shouted at Ardeshir. "If you want to see your father or your princess again, this is the time to prove it. These are not the people you want to please."

The bow felt awkward as he pulled the taut string and nocked the arrow. His first shots flew far wide of any target.

"Aim lower! Center the arrow on their belly and then release it."

The swarm of attackers seemed endless as the ambush transitioned to hand-to-hand combat. Several camels and two packhorses got separated and taken by the enemy.

And as quickly as it had started, the ambush ended.

Ardeshir dropped the javelin he had taken from Yas and placed a hand over his racing heart. His legs were weak and his breathing shallow. Sweat soaked him from his forehead to his belly.

The last combatants on horseback disappeared into the forest and the shouts of warriors quieted to reveal the wailing of traders mourning their losses.

Ten of the cataphracts roamed the hillside armed with spears, finishing off those enemy forces who were unable to escape. Five others recovered wounded members of the caravan and disposed of the dead into the river.

The losses had been significant. Five camels were taken and another proved too injured to save. They'd also lost a total of eight horses and two donkeys. Five warriors had been killed and seven more injured seriously enough that they would never fight again.

Yas organized the survivors and finished fording the river. She then gathered the warriors on the perimeter.

"Never again!" she shouted. "Never again will we be taken by surprise like that. We knew we were vulnerable there. Let's reorganize with crossbows out front and behind."

Once the camp was fortified on high ground and a security system established, Yas led twelve hand-selected cataphracts to chase down the raiders.

Ardeshir watched her go, wondering when he would see her again.

Every day Ardeshir watched for his sister's return, but five sunsets and sunrises passed before her plumed helmet appeared at the edge of the clearing where the caravan had made camp. Only ten of her warriors accompanied her, but at least they had three camels, two horses, and two donkeys still loaded with trading goods.

Ardeshir ran up to his sister. "What happened?"

Yas swung down off her warhorse. "They were waiting for us. We struck at night. We killed twenty, but they had already disposed of some of our animals and two of us were lost."

She accepted the gourd of fresh water he offered and drank greedily.

"We can't afford to take losses like this. Next time we will need better security and a better plan for crossing." She handed him a slingshot. "I forgot that this is something you used as a boy with the sheep and horses. Perhaps you could practice with it and get us something to eat."

He looked at the piece of leather lying limply in his palm.

"What good is this for a battle?" he asked.

In the following month, the caravan sustained four more attacks but suffered no further losses.

Every day, after driving the group hard from morning until noon, Yas held training routines for traders, warriors, and others who had accompanied them. The curriculum was filled with lessons on horsemanship, use of the crossbow, and hand-to-hand combat with knives, javelins, and swords.

At each river, they drove themselves to built rafts, set up crossing security, and moved as quickly as possible. Twice they carried out the procedure by moonlight.

They negotiated their way across Hindustan, through the tribal chiefs monitoring settlements in the Ganges and Indus River valleys, and allowed the caravan to resupply, refresh, and find strength for the last month of the journey.

Ardeshir ached more and more for the quiet realm of the emperor's garden where Liu had often shared tea. When musicians struck up their song and dance, his ears strained for a hint of the bone flute and the princess who had mastered it.

A week from Susa and home, while discretely washing in a tributary of the Karkeh river, Ardeshir relished the sweet waters of the Zagros mountains. These streams were sacred to Persian kings and their servants seemed to form a constant trail with their horse-drawn carts to transport water.

As he bathed, a young girl walked out of the bush and waded into the river with her hands outstretched.

"Do not come further," he warned, kneeling on the bottom to conceal his unclothed body. "Wait by the roadway."

But she continued up to her waist and only stopped when she was an arm's length from him. In her hand sparkled a brilliant blue lapis lazuli, a treasure sought in these mountains by the Egyptian Pharaohs.

"Leave it on the road and I will get it later," he said.

She cocked her head and examined his eyes. It was clear she didn't understand his speech. But of course no one around here would understand Mandarin. Why had he used it?

He adjusted his mind and instead addressed her in Farsi. "What is your name?"

"Farzana."

"Please wait by the road while I wash. I will see what you have to offer."

The girl smiled and turned around.

When he had dressed and reached the roadway, a dozen youngsters stood giggling in the bushes watching them. He felt something beyond humiliation with the knowledge that so many had observed his naked body.

"What do you want?" he asked, speaking first to the girl and then turning to include the other children. "Where are your families?"

The girl stepped forward with her offering. "We are orphans of war. We look after each other. We know the location of a cave of treasures nearby and offer this prize to you in exchange for your food and protection."

"What kind of protection do you need?" Ardeshir asked.

The girl held up the stone. "Bandits are hiding across the river, waiting for you to pass. They are also looking for orphans to enslave. We want to move to the orchards near Susa for winter provisions."

He found that the stone fit easily in the pocket of his robe, so he slipped it away and nodded for the group of youngsters to follow him.

"My sister leads the cataphracts who protect the caravan near here," he said. "My father has a farm near Susa and can provide all you need over the winter. Wait by the river and I'll come to you later to make arrangements for the crossing."

When he presented the proposal to Yas, she was agreeable to it—if the orphans provided sufficient treasure, they could tag along under the umbrella of her protection, at least until they reached the farm.

"I'm sure Father will be happy to have more pickers for the harvest in the orchard," she said. "No matter how many of these lost children we take in, though, there always seem to be more. You may not believe it, but after half a year on horseback I'm looking forward to some good walks and a nice bed."

The crossing took place two days later and proceeded without incident. The children fell into step with the donkey train, and occasionally a trader would drop his camel and scoop up a child for a bit of a ride.

Once they had skirted the bandits, the traders broke into song and the children joined in.

Three days from home, a band of cataphracts galloped up the road on their Friesian charges. The caravan's lead riders trotted out to meet them and exchange information. In a short time, one of the riders thundered back to convey a message to Yas, who had been in the midst of a lesson teaching Ardeshir how to ride while standing on the back of his mount.

"Captain!" the rider shouted. "Your father has left for Ephesus to reclaim his house there for use by the church he started. He instructed us to find you and let you know that you are to return and oversee the farm. If your brother is alive, he is to go north to be with his aunt for more training to assume his role as prince."

Ardeshir slipped off the horse. A great depth of disappointment twisted his gut, stifled his breathing, and robbed his legs of strength. He had returned for one reason: to gain reassurance from his father.

Yas dismissed the warrior and turned to her brother. "Well, it looks like we have a difficult situation. I have promised a thousand horses to the emperor. I have also promised that you would bring the horses to him. What are we going to do now?"

The cataphracts turned around and raced back down the road toward Susa, no doubt relieved that they wouldn't have to ride all the way back to the emperor's palace.

"I could ride after Father and help him reclaim his home and establish his church," Ardeshir said. "Maybe if I worked with him for such a cause, he would feel proud enough to honor me with respect."

Yas stepped up and backhanded him across the shoulder. "I didn't bring you home to have you pity yourself in front of orphans. Father will do what Father will do. He's a warrior who is searching for a reason to fight."

She adjusted the pack on her horse and waved at the lead rider up ahead.

"We will go back to the farm," she told her brother. "I will round up the horses and you will take them to the emperor. By the time you've accomplished the mission, you will have done something to make him proud. And who knows? Perhaps there will still be a princess waiting for you when you arrive."

Ardeshir's ensuing glare hardly fazed her smile.

"You know that her suitors must have claimed her by now," he said. "The only thing waiting for me is a general and a leopard. Teach me the way of a warrior and a prince and I will earn my respect wherever I go. I'm not ready to go to our aunt and be stifled in the court of the Magi."

Seven

The Friesian stallion heaved under him as Ardeshir stopped the beat's gallop across the plain. The Zagros mountains rose before him in all their snow-capped glory against a pale blue sky. Their silhouette reminded him of a giant lying on its back covered in a blanket of white. He could see the forehead, chin, neck at one end, and towering toes at the other.

Half a dozen cataphracts charged up behind him.

"Sir!" the lead horseman called. "We have pushed these horses as far as they can go."

Ardeshir climbed onto the back of his mount and stood balanced there as he surveyed the riders and the glorious scene around them.

"The emperor wants a thousand warhorses who will carry his men across mountainous terrain even rougher than ours," Ardeshir said. "I will not sell him animals that are weak and worthless. Call the trainers and have them bring us hardier stock."

"Sir, your sister is the one who sends us these horses from her excursions to the north. It would dishonor her to reject what she has chosen."

Somersaulting off the back of his horse, Ardeshir landed on his feet and walked toward the warrior. "Tell me, soldier. Who did my sister leave in charge while she was gone?" He unsheathed a curved dagger from his waistband and held it above his head. "Who is it that knows the mind of the emperor and the kind of warhorse he might desire for his army?"

The cataphracts all dismounted and ran their hands over the necks of their mounts, whispering calming words.

"We are men who care about only three things," the horseman replied. "Our land, our horses, and our poetry."

"Then spin me a poem to match the beauty of the mountains and the plain," Ardeshir prompted. "Spin me a poem that captures all the sun and the rain."

The cataphract guzzled from a gourd of water, clenched his fists, locked his knees, and cocked his chin as if imitating a statue.

"An emperor rode on horses of fire; nothing else marked his true desire; he smote all those who refused his empire; those who refused to call him sire."

Another cataphract stepped forward in a similar pose.

"An ancient one from the heart of the sun stopped one day for a touch of fun. He danced to the flute of his only son and did not stop 'til day was done."

The band of warriors broke into dance and clapping as others took their turn.

Finally, their leader turned to Ardeshir. "Prove yourself, my future prince. What have you brought back from the bed of the sun?"

Ardeshir executed a back flip and then hopped up to stand on the back of his mount. The surprised horse bolted and left him scrambling to hold his place. He slipped down, secured the reins, and brought it back to the group.

"By the pond of the koi she sat so still, rock hard mind and an iron will, dragon tongue of fire and eye to chill, hungry for a horseman to kill."

The men stood silently, unsure how to respond.

"That's what the emperor's daughter is like," he said. "Can you imagine the heart of the father?"

The leader nodded. "We will make sure the horses are ready for the journey and for battle."

Despite the depiction of his poem, Ardeshir's dreams at night haunted him. He saw the princess posed serenely in her boat on the pond, playing her flute, nodding at him, sending him paper messages to woo his attention.

The family home was lonely, with his father having taken his two brothers and younger sister to Ephesus. The shelters on the fringe of the farm housed a dozen mothers and twenty-seven children. Fourteen of these were orphans who depended on him for provision. Their hard work had brought in a rich harvest and the barns were full. For now, life remained peaceful.

The twelve new orphans who had joined him along the way often chaffed at the rigid discipline required of living in community. Integrating with the other orphans wasn't easy for them, but they did their work hard and remained loyal to Ardeshir. Farzana in particular displayed her loyalty at every opportunity and soon blossomed into a young woman—one who clearly had eyes for him.

One evening, as he struggled with his prayers, Farzana arrived with an armload of firewood. He had designated the task of gathering wood and keeping the fire to another of the new orphans.

"Where is Sanjay?" he asked.

Farzana knelt by the fireplace, laid the wood in its box, and bowed low. "Forgive my intrusion, my prince. Sanjay is ill and I offered to fulfill his tasks. I trust the sight of me doesn't displease you."

The sight of her hadn't displeased him at all. She had adapted the dress of the higher-class women on the farm. Her plaited hair featured a crown of strung pearls at the back and a triangular leather cap at the front. Gold bangles hung from her ears and a glittering necklace of lapis lazuli hung around her neck. A warm cape rested across her shoulders and the long flowing blue robe was banded around her waist by red cloth.

When she stood before him, hands open, he found himself suddenly speechless. The longer he stood in her presence, the more uncertain she became until tears ran down her cheeks.

Without warning, she turned and fled.

But for the next week, Ardeshir's firewood was always piled neatly by the back door of his home.

A week later Sanjay, returned to his tasks.

"Where is Farzana?" Ardeshir asked.

"She has returned to her work with the horses," Sanjay said. "I trust she did not displease you while I was sick. She begged me to give her a chance to serve you."

"She did not displease me. I need to find a way to thank her for her service."

In the meantime, his daily routines with the cataphracts kept his battle skills sharp. But without his sister, he lost some of his will to persevere through the increasing chill of winter; his exercises were short and his times by the fire long.

When a band of mounted militia from the Magi rode in, Ardeshir was unprepared to host them—or fight them, if necessary.

One of the house servants alerted him to their arrival.

"Set the tables and prepare a feast," Ardeshir ordered. "Call the other warriors and keep them alerted."

When the men of the militia had finished stabling their horses, Ardeshir stepped out of the warmth of his home to greet them.

"Greetings from all of us loyal to the empire," he called. "How is my aunt, the queen?"

The captain of the militia removed his helmet. "The queen is well, my prince. She desires for you to visit so she may assess your preparations for what comes next."

"Such a grand woman, the queen," Ardeshir remarked. "Come! Let us eat, rest, and talk. Indeed, I have much to say about what comes next."

During the meal, the leader of the militia nodded toward Farzana as she replenished the guests' plates.

"Who is this fine woman you hide in your stables and flaunt in front of us while our stomachs are hungry for food?" the leader asked. "Is she part of the hospitality you offer?"

The fire in Ardeshir's gut took him by surprise. He had a strong desire to please, but his desire to protect the young woman was stronger.

"She is not available," he said.

"Oh, so she is your consort." The man smirked. "I don't blame you. I would keep such a filly to myself as well. Who else is available among your stable of delight?"

"We are a people set aside for Yeshua. We practice abstinence until marriage and do not give our girls for pleasure."

The militia's leader furrowed his eyebrows. "What strange practices are you bringing to this land with your strange god. The gods have designed women for the pleasure of a man. We understand your father had strange ideas, too, but you are young and virile… and a warrior." He raised his golden wine chalice. "Surely you know by now the pleasure of the women who look to you for their provisions?"

Ardeshir stood and surveyed the warrior reclined below him. "You have come to discuss my future in the kingdom, not to discuss these girls or the faith by which my family provides for their care. You are welcome to finish your business, enjoy our lodging, and return to the queen in the morning."

With that, he left the room.

Later that night, a frantic knock on Ardeshir's front door awoke him from sleep. Sanjay stood outside in his night dress.

"My prince," the servant began. "I don't know where else to go."

"What is the trouble?"

Sanjay fell to his knees, sobbing. Finally he choked out his message. "The leader of the militia has taken Farzana in the stables and forced her to fill his pleasure. She called for help—but when I tried to intervene, the others held me back. I fear they will all take their turn with her if you don't stop them."

Ardeshir snatched up his javelin and sword as he raced toward the stables. There, he found the girl sprawled on a scattered bed of hay, her robe torn, her pearl crown broken, and the leather triangle headpiece lying on the floor.

The militia leader stood over the sobbing orphan with her torn robe. Another man appeared to be disrobing, as though to take his turn.

Ardeshir took three steps and ran his javelin through the back of one rapist, then swung his sword at the other.

"How dare you violate my girls and ravish what is not yours to have?" he demanded.

The leader fell to his knees and rolled over, his eyes frozen wide with surprise as blood gurgled from his gaping lips.

The other soldier backpedaled with his hands raised. "Whoa! I never touched her, my prince. She is only the stable girl. We are fulfilling our pleasure, as all men do."

Ardeshir waved his sword overhead like a wild man. "Go, wake the others. Leave this place now. Take your vermin back to their queen and leave us in peace."

Sanjay then knelt beside Farzana, weeping with her and covering her with a blanket.

"Go, call some of the women," Ardeshir ordered. "Tell them to clean her and put her in a room where she won't be bothered any longer."

Sanjay tore himself away from the girl and raced into the night.

Farzana clasped the top of her head with her hands, hiding her face as she wept. "I tried to stop him," she said. "I tried."

He knelt beside her, adjusting the blanket. "I know," he assured her. "I know."

She clasped his hand. "I want to die. You rejected me and now this. I have nothing to live for."

He sat next to her in the straw. "You're safe now. You're safe."

Two women rushed in and threw themselves onto Farzana. He withdrew as her sobbing intensified. What had he done?

Alone in his room, he pondered the fate that had befallen poor Farzana, and all because of his own hesitancy to respond to her clear interest. His father had trained him to respect women and never force himself on them. That was not the Way. The Way involved putting the best interests of others ahead of oneself. It involved mutual love and respect, granting value and peace and hope to those who looked up to him.

A small woven purse on the counter of his room caught his attention, and he dumped out its contents. Within it he found all the notes the Han princess had ever sent him.

"Come!"

"Follow!"

"Lu Hou. Come soon."

"Coward."

"Return what you have stolen."

The sum of his memories on five pieces of hemp paper. The first of them blurred into indistinct memories of their clandestine meeting at the gazebo under the vines. Her eyes had spoken in ways her notes could not.

With greater detail, he treasured the memory of the note in which she had revealed to him her name.

The word *coward* spoke for itself. He had failed her and proven to be a worthless teacher. A messenger claiming truth who had no truth to share.

But the last note made no sense. What had he stolen that he had to return? If he ever did go back, he harbored little doubt that his fate would land him in the hands of the general and the claws of the leopard.

Eight

On the third day of tracking an elusive goat in the Zagros mountains, Ardeshir spotted a messenger on the trail below him. He had expected another messenger ever since his killing of the first messenger after Farzana's rape. His aunt had ordered him to come to her; his refusal, plus his hostility so far, had meant an official sanction was inevitable. He couldn't expect to dispatch the queen's right-hand man without consequences!

To cover himself, he had drawn up a letter for his father and sent it by imperial post at considerable expense. It explained his time with the Han, the result of the trade mission led by Yas, the details of the horses she was collecting on behalf of the emperor, the incident involving his aunt's captain and Farzana, and the overall health of the farm.

But the letter wouldn't reach Ephesus for another ten days—that was, if his father had even arrived there. What would the latest news do for his reputation in that city?

He spotted the messenger trudging through the knee-deep snow without proper footwear.

"Messenger!" Ardeshir called to the man on the trail far below. "For the sake of peace, the one you seek can be found in Susa. Return there and wait for him."

The messenger halted in his tracks.

Ardeshir sheltered behind some trees, hoping to elude the man. The last thing he needed right now was for his aunt's men to keep hounding him. He set up a decoy trail, then doubled back on himself and skirted an outcropping of rocks and branches to reach a cave in which to duck out of sight.

By dusk, there was thankfully no sign of the messenger.

Ardeshir set out again, this time heading for the camp where he'd left his servants with the horses and supplies. When he arrived, he encountered the messenger happily warming himself by the fire.

Resigned to the reality of his situation, he stepped into the encampment. The messenger rose, handed him a vellum scroll, and then retired into a goatskin shelter he had rigged for himself. Not a word was needed.

Sitting on some rocks within the fire, a pot of goat stew simmered. The concoction was flavored with cinnamon, mint, and pomegranates. The tantalizing aroma made Ardeshir's stomach gurgle in anticipation and he sat on a wooden stool to await the meal.

After the soup, he indulged in stuffed fruits and vegetables before retiring for the day, thoroughly satisfied.

The messenger was gone by the time he emerged in the morning and still he hadn't read the message. At least it seemed that the queen was allowing him to appear before her of his own volition. He had expected that he might be swarmed by vengeful militiamen intent on taking him away from the farm. But perhaps his aunt was only waiting until spring when the journey was easier.

Two weeks passed and still he avoided unrolling the vellum. He slept in a different location each night in an attempt to create some space should the troops come for him when he was least alert.

What was taking his sister so long to get back with the horses? The weather storms pounded the settlement daily and he knew Yas would be without protection.

His irritability surfaced with several of the servants. One day he raged at Sanjay as the young man brought him an armload of wood for the fire.

"What's taken you so long?" Ardeshir demanded. "I'm almost out of wood. What have you been doing all this time?"

Sanjay knelt on one knee and bowed his neck. "I've been tending Farzana. There is little wood left in the homes and she's now expecting a child. She was feverish and needed a friend."

Guilt swept over him like a storm off the mountains. He sprang from the chair where he'd been warming his hands and rushed for his overcoat.

"Take me to her," he said. "The orphans I vowed to protect will not go unprotected."

Ardeshir hadn't been to the farm's outer shelters since he was young. When he got there, he found the snow packed high against the sides of the stone structures. He could see the gaps under the roofing where smoke escaped.

He stepped into the smoky interior, which made it hard to breathe.

"Where's Farzana?" he asked one of the girls blowing on the fire. "That wood is green, child. Where's the good wood?"

"It's all gone to your house and to the cataphracts," Sanjay said from behind him. "No one dared to use what was meant for you."

"Surely, there must be dry wood somewhere? Sanjay, go through all the buildings and tell me where the dry wood is. If you don't find enough, take a sleigh to the neighboring farm... or anywhere you need to go in order to get wood for the widows and orphans in these shelters. Charge it to me."

He turned to the girl who had been blowing the fire. She had backed into a corner and was cowering.

"Child," he said, taking a step toward her. "No one will hurt you. Show me Farzana."

A fit of coughing under thick blankets betrayed Farzana's hiding place. The smoke was thick and Ardeshir began to cough as well. He surveyed the room with distress.

"Wait right here," he said. "I'll be back soon. You're all coming to stay in my place. Hurry and pack your belongings and blankets."

It took half an hour to get the horses harnessed to a cart large enough to ferry the children and their belongings to the main house, but soon they were loaded and setting out across the farm. The little girl who had nurtured the fire now stood boldly on her tiptoes, feeling the rush of the icy wind on her face as the horses trudged through the snow.

Once the children had unloaded their supplies, they raced for the fireplace and huddled around it like puppies with a bone.

Ardeshir sought out Farzana when the horse was stabled and the cart put away. He sought her eyes and found them, inviting her with his chin toward a nearby chair.

She slowly dragged her blanketed bulk into place.

"Why didn't you tell me about the pregnancy?" he asked.

She hung her head. "I am ashamed."

"It wasn't your fault."

"You don't understand."

"Understand what?"

She shifted herself and looked him in the eye before finding the courage to speak. "I dreamed every night that it would be your child I carried." She awaited his reaction. Seeing nothing repulsive, she continued. "When you killed that man who made my baby, I couldn't imagine how I would raise a child without its father. I began to dream again that you might take this child as your own, but I couldn't explain what I would tell that child about why we lived so far away from you. Now you have taken us into your home. I don't dare sleep in case this is all part of a dream and I wake up back where I was."

Ardeshir looked into the dancing flames, and the images he saw tore at his imagination. The princess with the flute danced across his vision only to be swallowed by the queen coming like a dragon to swallow him.

Among those images wafted a young woman carrying a baby and holding it out to him for acceptance.

Tears trickled down his cheek as the image merged with thoughts of his own mother handing him over to a gladiator. His father. A man whom he wondered whether he could ever please.

All these children wanted was to be loved and accepted.

"You are safe here," he said to Farzana before getting up and walking out into the cold night wind.

Upon his return, the four orphan girls slept near the dwindling fire. Ardeshir stoked it with enough wood to burn through the night, then used a flame to light a clay lamp and headed for his room. As he set the lamp down on a small table, he spotted the rolled-up vellum. It was time to face the queen's message.

The seal had almost broken and he was surprised not to see his aunt's insignia pressed into the wax. With finality, he held the wax over the lamp's flame and watched the wax drip away.

Maybe I should wait until daylight when I can read it easier, he thought.

He laid it down and prepared his bed with its thick blankets of sheepskin. Images of Farzana huddled under her blankets in the thick smoke made him shudder, though, as he tried to sleep.

He finally rolled out from his bed and retrieved the scroll. To his surprise, it wasn't from the queen at all. The message came from his sister—and it hardly made any sense.

Temple of Fire. Ambushed. Horses taken. Broken arm.

At first this seemed like a setup to lure him into a trap. He wouldn't put it past the Magi to pull a stunt like that.

But as he examined the circumstances more deeply, the truth became evident. His sister had dictated this message to the very same messenger he had tried to avoid while hiding in the mountains.

Shame washed over him as he realized that his fear of his aunt may have cost his sister her very life.

Only hours later did the full reality of the situation sink in. Yas had been captured and the horses taken. After all, his father had warned him many times not to go near the Temple of Fire in Susa… but this time he would have no choice. His father wasn't around to intervene.

Prior to dawn, Ardeshir rounded up a dozen of the cataphracts and headed out at full gallop. The snow lay fresh over the countryside and provided a sense of peace and calm belying the reality ahead.

Armed with crossbows, lances, and swords he embraced, the advantage he would have in surprise. Five of his men knew the grounds of the temple from previous skirmishes with his father, so he allowed them to take the lead.

The group arrived just as the sun crested the hills. They slipped into the forests behind the temple and two of the men spied on the early morning activity, watching for security. They returned within the hour and reported that two dozen guards stood around the perimeter of the grounds. The men appeared lax, though. One of the spies drew a rough outline in the damp earth to demonstrate the approximate locations of the various buildings in relation to each other. Inside the main gate lay an ornate arch dedicated to the eternal flame. A stone's throw from there was a residence for the priestesses and other women who continually swept the grounds.

At the back lay an oval pool and white building which seemed to be given extra security. The men suggested that Yas was likely held inside.

"We'll go at night," Ardeshir said. "Spread out, hide your weapons and armor, and gather again when the sun sets. If they haven't killed her yet, they probably won't do it now… not unless they see us coming. Keep your eyes open for anything unusual and report to me here."

He spent the afternoon gathering branches and ferns. He also dug a shallow dip off the beaten path and covered it with forest debris. It would be his refuge if he needed to hide.

Halfway through the afternoon, one of the men slipped through the trees and caught his attention.

"It looks like there is a lot of extra activity among the priests near the oval pool and white building at the back of the property," the man reported. "Also there's been a cartload of extra wood dropped off by the arch of eternal flame. They may be preparing to sacrifice something tonight."

Instinctively, Ardeshir understood what—or rather, who—the sacrifice would be. But rescuing his sister wouldn't be easy.

He sent a messenger to round up the others for a quick planning session. The sun was kissing the horizon when the last warrior arrived.

The plan was simple. Six of the cataphracts with crossbows would approach from the perimeter near the women's residence. They would eliminate any security or priests who might attempt to take Yas to the eternal flame. Four of the men with swords and javelins would quietly take out the other security and prepare to raid the building where Yas was held. Two warriors would stay with him to nab Yas and get her away while the others carried out a decoy to lead pursuers in another direction. They would meet at the crossroads outside town on the way to the farm.

As dusk absorbed itself in shadows, a contingent of priests and militiamen stepped out of the white building by the pool. A solitary figure dressed in scarlet and black robes was escorted out. It was a woman, and she frequently stumbled and needed to be steadied by the priests. It appeared that they had drugged her.

As they rounded the pool, Ardeshir's men unleashed a sling of arrows. Four of the priests fell writhing while two of the security men cursed the arrows that had lodged in their arms and legs. Another round of arrows found targets in the two priests escorting the robed figure. They fell, but so did the woman.

Raising an alarm, the rest of the group scrambled back toward the white building.

Right then, four cataphracts blocked the stairs. Dozens of warriors emerged from hiding to block the bushes and buildings to defend the fugitives. The four cataphracts were significantly outnumbered, though, as they fought their way toward the perimeter.

Ardeshir and his two warriors raced into the pile of bodies by the pool and pulled Yas away. The chaos of fighting almost covered Ardeshir's retreat but a wounded soldier nearby cried out an alert. Their plans hadn't taken into account having to escape with a drugged and limp body.

The cataphracts with the crossbows arrived and systematically skewered those in pursuit of Ardeshir. The two men with him pivoted to fight off the first wave of enemy warriors, despite overwhelming odds. But they had known the risks.

Ardeshir carried Yas into the woods and headed for his hidden refuge.

"Over here!" a voice shouted moments after he had pulled the branches over them. "They aren't far…"

Yas moaned and he covered her nose and mouth with his hand, holding her body tight next to his. The footsteps crunching along the path quickly faded.

"Are you sure they're not hiding in the brush?" another voice called. "We should spear any piles of branches we come across. I've seen that done before."

"Don't waste your time. They've got to be just up ahead. He can't get far trying to carry her. We need to carry out the sacrifice before the full moon comes up."

A spear thudded into the ground inches from Ardeshir's head. He heard two more thuds nearby.

"Watch for footsteps in the snow," a warrior shouted.

Then their running feet pounded off down the path.

Soon after the full moon had reached its zenith, Ardeshir rolled out from under the branches and scouted the surrounding area. Satisfied that no one was near, he pulled Yas out. She was groggy but alive.

He stepped across the path that crossed near the temple and climbed the hillside into the forest on the other side. It took him until nightfall to reach the crossroads where he and his men had agreed to rendezvous.

Seven of his men were waiting at the appointed spot.

"Where are the others?" Ardeshir asked.

"They died like warriors," one of them reported. "I watched the militia make sure they were dead and throw them onto the eternal flame. They had their sacrifice. Just not who they wanted."

Yas gained alertness as they rode back in the direction of the farm, and by the time they arrived she was fully aware.

"What took you so long?" she said. "I sent you a note."

Ardeshir winced. "One of these days, you and I will have to share a few stories about the last few weeks."

Nine

Three weeks later, Yas's arm had healed enough for her to throw a knife and lift a javelin and so far none of the spies they had posted reported any movement by the queen to come after them. They had also received no word from their father.

The queen's messenger had clarified one thing in Ardeshir's mind. His aunt intended to bypass his father and nurture Ardeshir as the next sovereign, succeeding her. He couldn't imagine any way in which he could dishonor his father more.

Ardeshir sat on his mount slinging stones at trees, birds, and fenceposts. His release was smooth and he usually hit his target.

The farm had been fortified with taller fences and secure gates in the last few weeks, with tunnels dug between the stables, main hall, and shelters to protect residents from harsh weather and enemy attack. The outbuildings had been insulated with sheepskins on the walls and floors while the fireplaces had been repaired and the gaps under the roofs sealed.

Farzana had been staying in the main house with one other girl, but the two of them had recently chosen to return to the newly furbished cottage where they had come from.

Ardeshir and his sister took a ride one day up onto the ridge overlooking the farm. From here, they could see that the trees and scrub had been cleared from the perimeter. The threat of an ambush had greatly diminished.

"So tell me why it took you so long to come for me," Yas said. "They would have sacrificed me if you had waited one more hour."

Ardeshir smiled. He reached into the pack he had secured across his horse and tossed Yas an apple. "I see your arm is healing."

"You should have come sooner."

He shifted and waggled his neck a few times. "The truth is that I thought the messenger you sent had come from the queen. I didn't want to look at it. I nearly threw it away, in fact."

She tossed the apple core at his back as he turned and rode on. "Your fear nearly got me killed."

He shifted his mount to face her. "I always thought you were invincible. I never dreamed you might be captured or hurt. How did that happen?"

Yas looked away. "If I tell you what happened, you can't speak a word to anyone else."

"We are family."

She rotated her shoulders and settled in for the story. "I ventured near Dar, near the queen's palace. There, someone told me about fifty horses I could get from an old army post. I should have known better. I never realized that the queen might use me to get to you."

Ardeshir waited for more.

"Well, say something," Yas urged. "This is my first time playing the fool. You should tell me that you know how it feels or something."

All he did was smile with his chin in the air. "And it's my first time being the hero. I'm soaking it in."

"The deal seemed good, not to mention easy, so I only took two of my men to the army post. When we found the horses in a small field with no one around, we dismounted to take a closer look. Within a few minutes, we were surrounded by militiamen with their lances drawn. Of course, I tried to fight." She lifted her arm in the air. "I took out two of them but the rest piled on. My men were killed and my arm got broken. End of story."

"I think there must be more," he said. "When I found you, you were drugged and hardly able to function."

She hung her head. "They left me without food or water for three days. One woman who seemed friendly slipped by my dungeon under that white house and left some food and wine. I drank the wine before I realized it was drugged. After that, they kept me sedated."

"It's a good thing the Han general never saw you in such a state," Ardeshir remarked. "The princess herself would have scorned you."

"You really do have your mind fixed on her, don't you? It must tear you apart... Farzana here and the lotus flower princess over there..."

Ardeshir gripped the reins and kneed his mount forward, pulling up only inches in front of his sister. "I'm not the feeble-handed child you rescued there. Not anymore. I know how to fight. If you need proof, let's fight this out right now."

Yas threw back her head and laughed. "How brave you are, charging a woman with a broken arm. How noble to prove your honor by standing up for a princess who has been taken by feeble lovers. You think you're prepared for battle now that I've shown you how to ride a horse and throw a lance?"

She reared her horse, whose hoofs flailed as she urged it forward. Ardeshir recoiled as Yas swung down and jumped onto Ardeshir's mount. She wrestled him off the horse and he fell hard.

By the time he'd regained his breath, Yas was on his chest with a dagger at his throat.

"Have we proven ourselves now?" she said.

The ride home was quiet.

Five days passed before Yas again entered his home, this time with a peace offering of special Persian foods. He nodded toward the counter and returned to the carving he'd been working on.

"May there be peace between us," she said. "What is that carving? It looks like some kind of goddess. Don't we have laws against graven images in our faith?"

He set the carving aside. "As if you know anything about faith. I learned a few things from some master carvers at the emperor's garden."

She prepared a tray of fruit, flatbread, cheese, and some olives. "Here, this will take the edge off. I see that you're probably trying to carve an image of the princess. Apparently you can't stop thinking of her. Well, your fantasies are your own creation. Your own problem."

He popped a date into his mouth to break his fast. "Tell me about the teachings you heard at the Temple of Fire. I'm sure those priestesses tried to convert you in some way. What do they believe?"

She made up her own tray and plopped down cross-legged by the fire. "They teach about Zarathustra and the importance of truth." She added a chunk of wood to the blaze and shifted some of the embers under it. "There are twenty-one holy books, or nasks. Seven speak of law, seven of science, and seven of true religion. The books on law cover everything from family to public life, from farming to faith, from business to battles."

"So it's like the Torah... teaching us how to live?"

"Perhaps. I tried hard to avoid indoctrination." She grinned. "Remember, I'm the one who knows nothing about your faith."

"What else did you manage to remember?"

"Keeping the law seems to be a reflection of the nature of their supreme being. Somehow this law is designed to bring the divine and the human together. Their sacred texts are meant to defeat falsehood and draw out the sacred nature in each of us."

"Father told me a little about how distorted their thinking is when it comes to God."

"From what I understand, through teaching the masses the world will become a better place and we'll find our redemption." Yas rose and refilled her plate before returning to the fire. "Once I was drugged, I have no idea what they were saying. But in the first days, they made a sincere effort to focus my attention on some divine impulse that would arise if I understood true knowledge and reflected on it."

Ardeshir set his plate aside. "I've heard enough. The emperor's people teach something which they call 'the way.' These Zarathustrans teach another. The Jews and Egyptians teach yet other ways. From my time of thinking deeply on this, though, I've come to know that the Way is the way."

Yas stirred the fire again. "What does that even mean?"

"If you spent enough time in the emperor's garden, you would understand," he said. "I have work to do. Consider us at peace. Anyway, I can't believe we still haven't heard anything from Father after I sent him that message."

He was about to walk out the door when Farzana appeared, wrapped in a brown robe with a sheepskin draped over her shoulders.

"It's warm in here," the girl said. "Is it okay if I get something to eat?"

Farzana waited for his nod, then moved further into the room and looked over the tray that Yas had placed on the counter.

"I couldn't help but hear you talking," Ferzana mused. "What is this Way you mention? I've never had anyone teach about any of these faiths. I didn't even know there was a way."

"We'll talk when I get back." Ardeshir got up and walked toward the door. "I should have been teaching all of you, but I was so used to the teachings of Mother and Father that I didn't even stop to think that I could do it myself." He gestured at his sister. "But whatever you do, Farzana, don't listen to anything she tries to tell you about truth."

With that, he left.

Sanjay approached Ardeshir the next day as he brushed down his horse. "May I speak to you, sir?"

"Of course!" Ardeshir replied. "You're always welcome to speak as long as you have something to say."

Sanjay stood silently, furrowing his brow. "That is perhaps the problem, sir. I'm not sure what it is I am to say. Farzana says you will be teaching the others and I too wish to learn."

"You may come and listen to my teachings as long as your work is complete."

The air seemed to go out of Sanjay. "Sir, my work is never done." He picked up a broom and started sweeping out a stall. "Farzana and I were talking... and we want to know two things. Sir, we don't know what to call you. Should we call you Prince? Teacher? Master? Or just Ardeshir? We simply cannot know."

"You may call me friend."

"Ah, this is a good name." Sanjay swept the rest of the stall as Ardeshir threw in new hay and feed for his horse. "One more thing, friend. Farzana believes you may no longer wish to marry her now that she is with child. If this is so, would you be willing to bless my marriage with the girl?"

The question caught him off-guard. Of course he had never planned on marrying the girl, but the thought of losing her from his life altogether also hadn't been part of his plan. He was used to having her around and she made a good companion. She kept his house clean, made special meals, and knew how to draw him into deeper conversations.

"Sir," the servant prompted. "I mean, friend! Have I troubled you with my questions?"

Ardeshir gave his horse a pat. "I need to think about it. You and Farzana are both so young..."

He walked away, leaving Sanjay to hold the broom and furrow his brow again.

The sun shone brightly overhead and the last of the snows had melted off the roofs of the farm buildings. Meltwater trickled to the ground. The air was fresh, the blue sky studded with only a few clouds. All was well.

And as Ardeshir walked the ground, he certainly felt there was no hurry for children to rush into marriage. Look how long he himself had gone!

His dreams of the Han princess had been fewer since Farzana had moved into his home, that was certain. He thought of the unfinished carving he had been working on, then intentionally changed the direction of his thoughts to consider what it would mean to lose Farzana, a girl to whom he had attached his heart.

But the face of the princess with her flute never left his memory, even though it was no use. The princess's suitors had taken her.

He had a duty to complete before too long, though. He would finish rounding up the one thousand horses they owed the emperor, then deliver them and say farewell forever to the emperor's lands and the people in it.

As he rounded the corner to his home, movement in the forest beyond the perimeter of the farm caught his attention. It was the smallest reflection of sunlight on metal, but there was no mistaking what it meant.

He calmly picked up a basket lying in a snowbank and carried it back to the barn. When he arrived, he located Sanjay, who was just preparing to ride out.

"Friend, the militia has returned," Ardeshir said. "It seems the Queen will not be denied this time. Walk to the cataphracts and warn them to prepare for battle. And tell them not to look as though they're preparing. I'll warn the others to hide in the underground shelters. Take the underground tunnels and meet me back at the hall."

Hours after the men had gathered, one of the leading cataphracts approached him. "My prince, are you sure you saw evidence of the militia? Two of our men have walked the perimeter of the farm, pretending to check the gates. They have seen nothing."

Ardeshir walked to a nearby window and looked out. "They are there. They may be waiting for nightfall to storm us with fiery arrows, trumpets, and a blitz on our gates. Call my sister. She will be needed."

Yas arrived a few moments later and stared out the window alongside him. "You can feel them out there, can't you?"

"What else can we do?" Ardeshir asked. "Is there more we can do to prepare?"

Yas motioned to her captains. Over the next few minutes, they had set up a mock battlefield in the middle of the hall using plates, trays, cups, and lamps.

"They will try the main gate first," she said, indicating a plate along the simulated fence line. "We must meet them with crossbows and javelins of fire to keep them cautious."

"Where will we hide in order to surprise them?" asked one captain.

"We will collapse the roof of the tunnel that runs inside the gate from the hall to the stables," Yas said. "One set of archers will hide inside the trench. If they wait until dark, this trench will be hidden and serve as a pit for their horses. Another set of archers will shoot from the upper windows of the hall to divert their attention and make them think that is where we're hiding."

"The orphans and widows are safely in the underground shelters," the captain said. "My men will take our horses from the barn and create a diversion at the far end of the field to make them think we're preoccupied. Only twelve of us will be. They will believe we're weak enough to be easily overpowered."

Yas nodded and set a cup where the twelve would joust. "If it gets dark, build a bonfire there and pretend you're drunk. If these are only spies sent in advance of a larger attack, we'll give them no clear picture of our strength. And if this is the ambush, we will be ready."

Ten

For trained warriors, Ardeshir was surprised at how quickly the Magi's militia had been beaten back. It was strange to think about the fact he had been fighting his aunt's warriors who were trying to take him back to Dar to become the prince the nation craved.

Yas stood with him at the burned-out gate, examining the damage. "It doesn't seem like they came prepared to fight," she said. "When they launched those arrows onto the roof of the hall, we were fortunate that the snow was still deep enough to douse the flames. Our crossbows must have cut down twenty of their men as they reconsidered the price they were willing to pay."

Ardeshir helped move aside a charred post. "I wasn't surprised when they charged the gate, but I also didn't know if we could hold. They never even saw the trench… not until half a dozen of their men had already fallen in it."

He surveyed the field scattered with discarded helmets, shields, javelins, and pieces of armor.

"The forces you trained were ready," he remarked to his sister. "I'm impressed. I can see that I have a lot more to learn from you."

"What do we do with the bodies?" Yas asked. "On the battlefield, we would leave each side to retrieve its own dead. We don't want to leave them here, though, and invite them back for another round."

Ardeshir stood over one of the corpses. Two arrows were still embedded in the man's chest.

"I'll fix up a wagon," he said. "Put the bodies in the back. I'll drive it to Dar and talk to our aunt on my own."

Yas grabbed him by the elbow. "We lost four men and killed thirty of theirs. Why would you walk into the lion's den? If you're captured, what was the purpose of this battle?"

He scooped up a helmet and looked at the crest of the Magi's militia. "It shows that I'm willing to go on my own terms. If I am to be the prince this nation desires, I won't do it by force."

"I'll ride with you," she insisted. "I am your family."

Two dozen of the cataphracts rode with Ardeshir and Yas until they passed the crossroads at Susa. Sanjay had suggested the thirty bodies, piled above the gunnels of the wagon, be packed with snow to keep them from decay. A tarp contained the smell somewhat, but the blazing sun didn't help. Brother and sister rode with scented scarves over their faces.

The scouts for the militia spotted them when they came within a few hours of the queen's palace. One hour out, they were met by a large contingent of militia and Yas waved a white sheet above her head. The captain of the force sent half his men to check for others who may be concealed. Half surrounded the cart, then backed away when the smell became overpowering.

"Halt!" the captain ordered. "What brings you this way and what do you have in the cart?"

Ardeshir responded. "This is a mission of mercy. We're returning the men who perished in the mission to our farm. My sister and I come of our own free accord to see the queen."

The captain reined his horse in front of them. "You can't see the queen with this stink on you. My men will take over the cart while you bathe yourselves until you're presentable."

The man pointed at two of the militiamen; neither looked pleased to have drawn the assignment.

"We can finish what we started," Ardeshir said. "What chance is there that we might see the queen if we leave this cart?"

The captain drew his horse closer. "You do have a choice. You can ride on my men's horses or my men will take this cart with two extra bodies on board."

The ride to the palace on borrowed horses passed quickly. Once there, Ardeshir and Yas were given rooms with tubs of warm water to scrub and change into alternate clothing.

When they were seated in the grand hall, the imperial minister of the realm of Susa and Babylon met with them.

"The queen is on a mission to meet her brother," the minister declared pompously. "The timing of this visit is neither appropriate nor planned. If you are to be seriously considered for future roles in the realm, you must know that we Persians are a proud and free people who don't take the death of our defenders lightly."

"I'm assuming you don't take the spilling of royal blood lightly either," Yas said.

A grand marshal standing near Yas backhanded her across the mouth. She staggered, then lurched back at him. Before she could strike, she was grabbed by two courtiers. She stood her ground stiffly following a brief struggle.

The minister strolled up to Yas and scowled. "While you may have been taken in out of pity by our future prince, we know you're a worthless commoner destined to perish in battle. If you don't hold your tongue, we will feed it to the dogs. The Magi hold the power in Persia while we await to declare our King of Kings."

Ardeshir stepped forward and bowed as if to the Han emperor. "Forgive us, Minister, for overstepping the grace of your hospitality. Not all of us have been trained in understanding the powerful role of the Grand Senate, with its nobles, prelates, grand marshals, imperial ministers, and secretaries, to keep our great land stable."

The minister stepped away from Yas and faced Ardeshir. "What is this strange practice of bowing the head that I see in our future prince? And what are these strange words regarding forgiveness? What you need is a good lawyer to defend you for the havoc you have wreaked." He strolled back to the golden chair on the dais at the front of the room. "The queen has requested that you be sent to meet her at Damascus. She and your father are meeting with others who are planning to provide teaching of some kind. If the queen hadn't expressed the urgency of this matter, you would both be exiled, imprisoned, or worse."

Ardeshir bowed again. "Does it please the minister to supply us with horses and escorts to take this journey?"

The minister beckoned one of the courtiers to his side. "Let it be recorded that the woman known as Yas will be held in confinement at the palace until Prince Ardeshir completes his mission and returns to verify his place in the realm. Let it be recorded and let it be said."

Two of the security forces shackled Yas and dragged her from the room.

Ardeshir's mind worked overtime as the carriage in which he rode jostled along the rough road to Damascus. Thanks to the treaty between the Parthians and Romans, the militia handed off the escort of the caravan to a cohort of legionnaires at the border of Armenia.

Although the usual three-month trip by camel had been reduced by half, every bone of his body hurt and he eagerly alighted at each stop when the four horses were changed.

What was Yas enduring while he journeyed freely? How were Farzana and Sanjay faring as her baby's birth grew near? How was the princess doing with her new husband? How was Liu making out under the eye of the general and his leopard?

While the militiamen had treated him with grudging respect, the Romans made it clear that he would be on his own if they were attacked. The Romans' fee for this escort clearly needed to be renegotiated! Only once this was accomplished did the escort display more deference and determination to get him to his destination.

The city of Damascus was a walled fortress on a high plateau about two days' journey from the great sea. The mountains supplied water through the Barada River and the nearby crossroads—connecting Egypt to the south, Asia Minor to the northwest, the great sea to the west, and the Euphrates River to the east—provided the lifeblood of trade.

With hours to go, the roadway was already filling with carts, camels, caravans, horsemen, and people on foot.

When they were half an hour from the city gates, a community of tents and makeshift houses sprouted from the parched earth. Despite the spring runoff from the mountains, it seemed the river struggled to supply the demands of the population here. Farms tapped into the water for irrigation and others claimed its nourishment for their flocks, cleaning, and personal needs.

Their Roman escort eased the rigorous inspection they endured at the city gate and soon their carriage arrived in the marketplace, only slightly after noon. The Via Recta, or Straight Street, provided a clear compass from east to west through the city.

With a wave, the centurion who had provided security left them on their own and led his men deeper into the warren of basalt block buildings and habitations.

Greek, Aramaic, and Latin seemed to be the lingua franca of the marketplace and Ardeshir's Farsi and simple Mandarin seemed out of place. Vendors chattered at him, but their words were meaningless to his ears.

Finally, he spotted an oriental-looking seller of silk and jade. Marching confidently toward the canopy, he greeted the man in Mandarin. The surprised look on the vendor's face erased hours of anxiety and confusion.

"Welcome to my stand," the man continued in Mandarin after his greetings. "What may I provide you with on this fine day?"

"I am looking for my father and his sister," Ardeshir said. "They are Persians, darker and taller than me."

The vendor smiled. "Many people from many different places come to this market. You seem old enough to take care of yourself. How did you come to speak my language?"

Ardeshir scanned the crowd for any evidence of other Persians. "I lived in the emperor's palace gardens for two years, teaching his daughter about truth. I'm not sure what I accomplished, but I did learn to speak."

"Are you the Persian whose sister killed the three Yamoto to restore honor before the general?"

"Yes, it is me," he answered.

"I am the cousin of the gardener, Liu," the vendor said. "I was there when the battle happened. Your sister is famous now. How is she doing?"

Ardeshir shrugged. "She was taken hostage by the queen's forces in Persia, and I'm on my own mission. I must find my father and aunt in order to secure her release."

"She was such a great warrior. The princess has been in mourning ever since you left."

"What do you mean?" Ardeshir asked. "The princess is happily married to her suitor, isn't she?"

"The princess rejected all suitors and waits for one who will bring horses for the emperor. Many are working hard to bring her these horses."

His heart skipped. Who else but himself could this man mean? Was anyone else contracted to bring horses to the emperor?

There was no time to waste. He had to find his father and his aunt, secure Yas's release, collect the horses, and get back to the emperor's palace.

The vendor tugged on Ardeshir's robe. "There is a Persian by the fountain looking toward the gate. Perhaps that is who you are meant to find."

Ardeshir made his way to the fountain, where he encountered a muscular warrior whose broad chest boasted an armored vest. The man moved with grace for a tall man and rotated slowly, scanning the marketplace.

At last the warrior's gaze landed on Ardeshir. Seeing him, he signaled with his hand and approached. With practiced respect, he nodded and grasped Ardeshir by the elbow.

"I am Arsama," the man said, introducing himself.

"Ah, yes," Ardeshir responded. "The hero of strength. Your family named you well."

Arsama chuckled. "It was truly my uncle who saw my name and told me I must live up to the faith of my family. Now I am here to learn from your father about how to be strong in a new faith I knew nothing about. I understand you are learned in the truth of the Way."

Ardeshir fell into step with the warrior as they headed toward the gate. "I continue to learn each day. When you step into the Way, it's like falling into a bottomless well. The more I think I understand, the less I realize that I know."

"Truly it is a mystery,"

"Is my father close?" Ardeshir asked.

Arsama shook his head. "Perhaps you have not heard. Your father had to press on to Caesarea with the queen. They went to meet an apostle named John for further teaching. They are hoping to go with him to Ephesus to build a church."

Ardeshir stopped in his tracks. "When did they leave? I don't think I can bear another moment in a carriage on these rough roads. My sister needs me to return to Dar as soon as possible, to secure her release…"

"They left five days ago and I've come looking for you every day since. You can wait here, for they plan to return in two weeks. Although they might decide to go on to Ephesus. If so, I don't know when they'll be back. It's a two-day ride by horse to Caesarea, so you could eat and rest tonight and then leave in the morning."

Ardeshir stretched and rubbed his stiff hip. "I guess two more days is worth the trouble. Show me where to stay and where to eat."

Eleven

At Caesarea, Ardeshir got his first glimpse of Roman warships. The searing rays of the sun reflected off the sea and burned his retinas as he tried to shade his eyes and take in the sight of the towering masts. Men ran like ants over the rigging and deck, preparing for launch. Four rows of oars protruded from one side ready for action. Gulls drifted lazily under the azure sky.

The dilapidated buildings on the south side of the bay anchored an aging dock which appeared too fragile to hold the many crates, fishnets, and baskets of fruits waiting to be shipped. Freighters anchored in the harbor, waiting their turn for loading and unloading. The tang of sewage, kelp, and low tide hung in the air, mingled with the smoke of fires crackling along the shoreline.

"Come!" Arsama called. "We need to check in at the inn before we find them."

The inn's whitewashed exterior showed the dirt of decades of weather wear. Vines grew over the red-tiled roof and trailed down the back.

Inside, an ancient Hebrew man with two missing front teeth sat behind the desk, grinning.

"A Perthian," he lisped. His blue-patterned robe looked Persian in its weave and quality; his faded silky red turban, perhaps Indian. "Where from?"

"Susa," Ardeshir answered.

"Thutha, how nith." The innkeeper waved at a slave and showed him four fingers before adding, "Baths are free."

The slave picked up their bags and nodded for them to follow.

Nothing but a rough curtain served as a door to their space, and the straw pallets on the floor were well worn, but for now at least it was theirs.

The baths and the massage were heaven-sent, and a dinner of lamb shank, rice, flatbread, and tomatoes settled their stomachs. The wine eased their throats.

"When do we see my father?" Ardeshir asked as they lay down for the night. "I want to meet him first thing in the morning."

"I've sent a message to alert him that you're here. Once he knows everything is safe, he'll send a messenger to let us know where we can meet," Arsama said. "There's been a little trouble I haven't told you about."

"What do you mean?" Ardeshir asked as he plumped up his pillow and lay down. Every muscle in his body rebelled despite the massage. "Why didn't you say something before now?"

Arsama trimmed the wick of the lamp near his bed and watched it flicker. "Some of your father's old enemies didn't like his faith and gave him some trouble. He had to evade them for a short time. Your aunt is calling on some of her allies to intervene."

Ardeshir sat upright, throwing off his blanket. "My father is in trouble and you say nothing? What is my aunt going to do so far from home? You better not be leading me into some kind of trap."

Arsama rested with his back against the wall. "They told me not to say anything. They assured me everything would work out fine. Your father wanted to help reestablish the church in Ephesus, but he became sick and couldn't take the journey with the apostle."

Pacing the room solved nothing. Three steps one way and three steps another. Back and forth.

"I need to go out for some air," Ardeshir announced. He reached for his robe and slipped into it.

"No!" Arsama grabbed the edge of the robe. "The darkness is dark for a reason."

Ardeshir tried to yank the robe away. "What are you saying?"

"Drunken sailors, bandits, cutthroats, women of the night… it's no place for a prince who has been protected on a farm away from insanity."

"Insanity? You call this insanity? This is nothing compared to man-eating leopards, koi ponds, Yamoto fights, ambushes, and militia raids. In the face of insanity, all I need to do is breathe."

He yanked free and stepped through the curtain.

Arsama was still pulling on his robe as he followed. "The security man outside will stop you."

"Let him try. My sister has shown me a few ways to handle close combat."

The tussle with the guard was nothing compared to the melee with the band of sailors he and Arsama soon had to fight off. It was going so well until one of the sailors pulled a knife; Ardeshir kicked him in the knee, then elbowed him in the jaw, toppling him.

But that only attracted more brigands to join the battle. Arsama fell under a mob of five pugilists, abandoning Ardeshir to deal with the fury of a dozen others thrilled to the kill.

His first efforts downed three men, but the others pressed in from all sides. There was nothing he could do to help Arsama, so he backed toward a warehouse, trying to shield himself from attack on his blind side.

Without warning, someone grabbed him by the collar and pulled him back into the warehouse. Three strangers brandishing scimitars suddenly emerged from the building to block the mob from entering. Their weapons flashed in warning while the threats and yelling continued.

Once the mob had dispersed, one of the swordsmen dragged Arsama into the flickering light of two olive oil lamps. His face was hardly recognizable; his nose had been broken and blood smeared across his cheeks and forehead. His eyes were already swelling shut. Mercifully, the warrior was unconscious.

One of the swordsmen brought water and washed Arsama's face. Another adjusted the big man's broken arm and attached a crude splint.

Ardeshir heaved for air as he sat on a small crate of olives. "Who are you all?"

The swordsman who had attached Arsama's splint stood up. "We are protectors of the vulnerable, assigned by Rome to right what is wrong. We are thespian assassins who know who you are and why you are here." He stood up a little straighter. "I am known as Alexander, the healer. The one wiping the blood is Hermes. The brute is Tertullian. If we speak our true names, we lose our tongues."

Hermes, a warrior with the powerful shoulders of a giant, held out the blood-stained washcloth. "Why are you out in the night?"

"I thought you already knew everything," Ardeshir said.

"We know you are here for your father and your aunt," Alexander said. "Your father was the Roman emperor's champion in Ephesus and won the favor of our own teacher, Titius. We have lived on the stories of their past glory. But now we see he is old and frail."

Ardeshir's face hardened. "Where is my father?

Alexander pointed toward Arsama. "Perhaps we should attend to your companion first. Whatever reason you had for stepping out into the night, unprotected, it displays a lack of wisdom. You are no longer in Persia where people may respect you."

Ardeshir slammed his hand on the crate and staggered to his feet. "Respect? The Magi threw my sister in a dungeon so I could crawl here to my aunt and do her bidding. I was once sent all the way to the end of the Silk Road to prove myself and faced nothing but humiliation when I got there. There is no respect."

Tertullian, who had been standing in the doorway, now turned to face him.

"If you whine like a child, you will never be respected." Alexander raised his sword for emphasis. "If you flaunt your restlessness by reckless actions in the face of danger, you will never live long enough to gain respect. If you are ungrateful that others have risked their lives for yours, you will find yourself alone, unwanted, and unprotected."

Tertullian walked up to Ardeshir, towering over him.

"All I know is that your companion over there has paid a brutal price for being with you," he continued. "I have no doubt it was you who put him in this situation. Your foolishness may have made our mission to find your father much harder."

"What are you talking about?" Ardeshir asked. "What have you got to do with my father?"

Tertullian lowered his weapon. "Your father was taken by forces opposed to his faith. We were asked to intervene. No one knew we were here until we had to expose ourselves to protect you."

Ardershir sat down, stunned. His father had been taken? And now his father might be lost because of his own recklessness?

"Where's my aunt?" he asked, putting two and two together. These were the allies Arsama had told him about.

Tertullian moved back to his post at the door.

Hermes, still kneeling by Arsama, replied. "She is under the protection of two of our number. She is in disguise. We intended for you to meet her in the morning to explain what has happened. Now there is much uncertainty."

"Take me to her," Ardeshir insisted.

"Are you not listening? You and your family are in danger. Bringing you together could mean the end for both of you."

Ardeshir paced across the warehouse floor. "What am I going to do? My sister is in a dungeon, but I can't go back until I've met with my father. And you say he's missing?"

The three warriors waited in silence, one staring out into the darkness, another wiping Arsama's brow, and the other shuffling through a crate of fruit.

Finally, Alexander tossed an apple in Ardeshir's direction. Ardeshir caught it and polished it on his tunic.

"So what are you going to do?" Alexander asked.

"What choices do I have?"

The warrior took a bite of his apple and chewed slowly. "I see three possibilities. Stay and look after your companion here on the floor. Find someone else to look after him and go back to Persia and explain why your sister should be released." He took another bite. "Work with us to find your father."

Tertullian stepped away from his post at the door. "We can't afford to be hampered by someone who clearly has no thought for his choices. We don't even know where to start looking. Dragging him along won't help. Besides, look at him! How is a dark-skinned, bald-headed, clumsy oaf going to pass himself off as one of us?"

"I did watch him get in some good kicks and punches," Hermes said. "He has clearly learned something." He used his fist to hammer down the lid of a crate and then pried up another. "He could provide some interesting bait to draw out the conspirators if we stay close. Now that our presence is known, what point is there in trying to hide? There might be no better place to disguise ourselves than in plain sight."

"What would be the plan?" Alexander asked.

"One of us would walk openly with the prince, acting as if we're looking for the queen, asking vendors and anyone we met for help. That would make them think we don't know where she is." He bit into an orange and tossed one to Tertullian. "You take the wounded one somewhere for care, then slip away to warn the others of what's happening. I'll link up with another assassin, disguise ourselves as dockworkers, then pick up any talk on where the emperor's former champion has been taken."

"Meet back here each night, an hour after the sun goes down," Tertullian said. "I don't want to be the one to pamper this foolish one, but I suppose I must. He better not create trouble. If he does, I might be the first one to put a javelin through him."

Tertullian turned to Ardeshir and pointed toward some sacks of grain along the edge of the warehouse.

"Get some rest over there and we'll leave as soon as the sun comes up. That should be anytime now…"

71

Dawn was still a distant hope when the butt of a javelin poked Ardeshir in the ribs.

"Get up, we need to go," a voice said from the darkness.

"I don't even know what to call you," Ardeshir said. "I don't even care if it's your real name. I just need to get your attention somehow when it matters."

"Tertullian will do. Now get up, prince."

The pair was several streets from the harbor when the first fingers of dawn traced a crease through the night. They were dressed in plain brown robes with no head coverings, the disguises taken from a stock at the back of the warehouse. Their sandals also bore no mark of distinction.

Vendors were setting up shop as slaves waited in line to purchase supplies for their master's households. Traders moved their carts toward the docks.

"Watch for the street rats trying to con you into taking a tour of the gates of Hades," Tertullian warned. "They'll try to distract you at the slave auction and then rob you blind. Either that or they'll swarm you with numbers and hope one of them gets lucky."

Tertullian may as well have been a prophet, since a group of children, around ten to thirteen years of age, jogged around the corner right at that moment and began to dance and swirl around the two men.

"Hey giant, why don't you reach up and drag down a cloud for me?" one of the girls mocked them. "Why don't you cover that head before I'm blinded by the reflection of the sun?"

The boys darted in and out, slapping and laughing as if playing a game.

The oldest boy stepped in front of them. "Let me take you on a tour of the house of pleasure. A place beyond your wildest dreams. Fresh girls are ready and waiting."

"Walk on!" Tertullian picked up the pace so the leader of this gang of street rats had to change his tactics.

"Special price for you friends," the boy said, walking quickly alongside them. "Hey, I'm hungry. Why don't you spare me a shekel so I can get something to eat? Look, I have all these poor children to feed… you wouldn't want these orphans to starve to death, would you?"

When neither of the men responded, the boy lowered his shoulder and ran straight for Ardeshir. A dozen others swarmed from behind.

Tertullian was on them like a wild dog, tossing and throwing the children away.

When the group dashed off in search of other prey, Ardeshir bent over, breathing heavily. "Thanks," he said. "It didn't seem right to hurt children."

"It's not right for them to hurt you either," Tertullian said. "I wonder how long you would have stood there letting them try to rip away your robe and purse. Show me you have a sliver of manhood in there somewhere. It might make it easier to avoid the shame of being seen with you. Come, I think I know where we can find your aunt."

Twelve

His Aunt Laleh proved to be right where Tertullian said she might be: in the governor's mansion. After being forced into better robes by the household staff, Adeshir was permitted inside. The creases on the queen's face made her look older and frailer than he remembered. Why had he feared this woman? Although her elegant robes and flashy diadem demonstrated some effort at dignity, few outside her own security showed more than superficial deference to her.

"Where have you been?" his aunt asked. "We waited for months with no word from you. News from Ephesus was so bad that your father tried to go ahead. We've heard nothing since."

Ardeshir bowed on one knee and lowered his head. "My queen, I had important work to do. I tried to defend myself from what seemed like hostile forces." He rose at the flick of her wrist. "I am here now. How did my father become ill? How did he disappear?"

The queen waved the others in the room away. When the room cleared, she motioned him to sit beside her.

"He was sick with fever. The physician treated him with potions, but he only got worse. He called for the apostles in Yerusalayim, but they couldn't come." She passed to him a tray of dates and figs. He took a small handful. "We aren't sure whether he was taken or managed to talk some sailors into taking him to Ephesus. A vendor has said he was seen being carried on a stretcher toward the harbor. No one there seems to remember much."

"I met some of the thespian assassins assigned to track him down," Ardeshir said. "They have heard several stories."

"What have they heard?"

"He was taken by forces opposed to our faith. That is what they believe." Ardeshir paced the room as he ran through the various rumors. "One heard that he was taken to Yerusalayim for healing by the leaders of the Way. Another reported that he had been killed by wild dogs when his body was dumped in the forest. Still another said he went off with the zealots to lead a rebellion against Rome."

"You can't believe anything you hear these days," the queen said.

A commotion in the hall created enough disturbance that she stood and sheltered behind her chair. Ardeshir positioned himself in front of her just as a dozen men poured through the curtained doorway.

The new arrivals stood with their heads bowed, hands over hearts.

"What is the news?" the queen asked.

A burly man with a greying beard and generous belly stepped forward. "Your majesty, we have news of some of the leaders of the faith you follow."

"What news?"

"Two men, known as apostles, have been martyred by Rome. "The one known as Paul has been beheaded. The one known as Peter has been crucified upside-down. There is a fury against the members of the Way and we have been asked to escort you back to Persia before the trouble extends here."

Ardeshir stepped forward. "We cannot go without my father, the queen's brother. Find him and we will go."

The man furrowed his brow when the queen nodded a confirmation of these orders. He then bowed and withdrew with the rest of the entourage.

"There will be no place to hide soon," the queen said. "I'm old and have no urge to travel without my brother. Return home and claim your honor, Ardeshir. I will send you my blessings so my men will honor you."

Ardeshir stepped to the curtain and drew it aside to find a man who had lingered to overhear their conversation.

"I believe we are in need of privacy." Ardeshir waited for the man to nod and move away down the hall. He turned back to his aunt. "I cannot go until I know the true story of my father. I've been away from him too long and need his blessing. My sister has promised that I will take one thousand horses back to the Han emperor, but I need to know if this is my father's desire as well."

Queen Laleh smiled at him. "Your father adores his son. He spoke of little else during our travels. Whatever you believe is best for our nation, he will bless it."

A clash of weapons echoed in the hall and the queen grasped Ardeshir by the shoulders.

"There is trouble. Go now, out the back way through those curtains." She pushed him toward the right side of the room. "Return to your escorts and take shelter until you hear of my fate. The glory of our nation rests in your hands."

One hour later, he was still running, lost in the alleyways of the city. The stench of rotting sewage, unwashed humanity, and human waste hung like a putrid blanket around the mudbrick homes. He ran past beggars, zealots, vendors, and sailors, ignoring all their pleas for help. Barking dogs chased him on several occasions and he kicked them away.

As he passed a well, a young woman pulled up a small bucket and filled her four gourds. She wore a simple tunic with a light vest and a tattered shawl.

He stopped next to her, exhausted and breathing heavily.

The woman eyed him a moment, then extended a gourd. "Are you training for Caesar's games, or can you take a moment to quench your thirst?" she asked with a smile. Her Aramaic was pristine. "I see you are dressed to see the governor, yet you run as if your life depended on it. Have you killed someone?"

He took the drink. Guzzling greedily, he emptied the gourd down his throat, then poured the remainder over his head, before handing it back. He wiped his mouth with the back of his hand.

"I have harmed no one," he said in simple Aramaic. "I only seek shelter from someone who might want to harm me."

"I see by your speech that you are a foreigner," she said. "Should I fear for my life or offer you refuge in my family home?"

He scanned the neighborhood. "Should I fear for my life at your offer or should I be grateful that you value hospitality to a stranger above your own life? I don't have much coin if that is your desire."

She lowered the bucket and refilled the gourd. "You can keep your coin. Our faith in the God of Abraham, Isaac, and Jacob sustains us. We have everything we need."

Ardeshir lifted two of the larger gourds and nodded. "It would only be for the night. I have somewhere to be in the morning. I trust your abba will not run me through with a sword by showing up with his daughter?"

She picked up the other two gourds, tipped one back to drizzle into her mouth, and chuckled. "My abba would probably do just that... if he were living. It's only my mother and myself. We wait for my brother to return with his wages from the harvest. You can use his pallet in exchange for cutting our wood and feeding our chickens."

Although the walk to her home was short, Ardeshir constantly looked over his shoulder. He was relieved when they ducked into the small mudbrick structure with the thatched roof.

The woman's mother welcomed them with a smile as inviting as her daughter's. The cool interior of the home offered a great respite from the heat and he allowed the woman to wash his feet as he eased himself onto a stool.

She disappeared into an inner room and returned with an old carpenter's tunic.

"Here!" she said. "This will work better when you cut the wood and feed the chickens. Dinner will be waiting for you when you get back. The neighbors will watch everything you do, so don't act suspicious."

"How will I explain my presence?" he said.

"You are my brother's friend. You've come to help us with our chores. If you work well enough, you can tell them you have come to betroth me." She laughed with a timbre that reminded him of Yas. "I love to hear these hags talk around the well as if they know every secret in town. Now go, unless you have brought the dowry."

The stack of wood was larger than Ardeshir had hoped and his hands were more tender than he realized. Despite the growing blisters, he smiled through the chore and found himself imagining what a life in this city would be like with a pleasant wife.

A pang struck him as visions of the Han emperor's daughter intruded into this fantasy. The princess sat motionless with her bone flute in a simple boat on the pond.

He chuckled as he envisioned her falling into the water.

"What humors you about chopping wood," a voice asked. It was the woman.

He was glad his own skin was dark, for he was sure his cheeks burned even darker at having been caught.

Ardeshir continued to chop. "I enjoy the dreams of my mind to distract me from the pain in my hands."

He showed her the blisters, several of which had already broken.

"Were your thoughts of me?" she asked, ignoring his hands.

He set the hammer down and flexed his fingers. "It would be hard to deny that your face flitted across my mind. I would appreciate some cool water for my hands, if that is possible."

She pivoted and fetched a small gourd from inside the home, then poured a small pool of water into his palms and waited as he rubbed them together. He bowed his head as she poured another small amount on the back of his neck and head.

"That's enough. The neighbors will do more than gossip if I have to go back to that well already." She paused to regard him. "Are your parents as dark as you?"

He stood back, eyeing her. Could she be sincere, ignorant, or merely making conversation?

"My abba is darker and my ima is lighter," he replied. "What else do you need to know?"

"How dark is your sister? You do have a sister, don't you?"

He pursed his lips and nodded. "She says she is lighter than the dusk and darker than the dawn."

"Hmmm. That sounds nice. How dark would our babies be?"

"Does it matter?"

She shrugged. "No, just wondering. My mother says sometimes I ask too many questions."

"Just don't ask questions in front of her that make her worried that I'll run off with you. I have many things to do while I'm here, but I promise not to take you from your mother. She needs you."

The woman nodded. "You're right! I guess she does. Maybe you'll come back in a few years and marry me."

"We will see what the God of Abraham, Isaac, and Jacob decrees," he said. "By the way, what is your name?"

"Mariam. And who are you?"

"Ardie," he said, shortening his name.

When the wood was finished and the chickens were fed, he dipped his hands in a basin of water and slowly washed them clean.

Mariam's mother wrapped his hands carefully. "You are not used to such hard labor," she remarked. "I hope my daughter didn't drag you home with promises she cannot keep."

"She only promised me a pallet and a meal in exchange for the wood and the chickens."

"Then sit, eat. That we can give you."

Ardeshir entertained them through the meal, and afterward, with stories of the Han emperor's garden and life in Persia.

He then swore them to secrecy. "You cannot tell a soul about my life," he said.

"Don't worry, we won't," Mariam's mother said. "No one would believe us. You do know how to tell a good story, though. If only such places would exist, we would move there in a moment."

The chatter in the streets slowly dimmed as the coolness of night sifted through doors and windows to quieten the souls of the weary. Even the rancid scent of the chicken coop, decaying vegetation, and unwashed bodies faded as he took up his dream of the emperor's garden. Was it all a dream, never to be seen again? Had he imagined a fantasy beyond the possibility of reality?

The smile of the princess handing him the hemp paper carried him through the darkness.

At first light, Mariam's mother placed a cup of tea at his door along with a large chunk of freshly baked flatbread. The scent of baking filled his senses and covered everything else.

After rising, washing, and eating—not to mention, getting directions toward the harbor—he changed back into the robe he had been given to see his aunt and the governor. He bid his farewell, then headed back in the direction of the docks.

"Don't forget me," Mariam called after him.

He backpedaled and waved. "Don't worry, Mariam. You are unforgettable."

Thirteen

It was amazing how short Tertullian could make himself seem when he bent over with a walking stick and shuffled his way through a crowd. In fact, the variety of disguises used by the seven thespian assassins surprised Ardeshir as the warriors came and went from the warehouse. From dockworkers to sailors to blind men to veiled women to rabbis to Roman legionnaires, there was no limit to what they could do and who they could be. Their facility with languages and voices boggled the mind.

Weeks had passed since Ardeshir's father had been abducted and hope was running out. Queen Laleh had disappeared from the governor's mansion as well and there was no word on the street as to what had happened to her. Their best lead seemed to be that a vendor had witnessed four men carrying a large stretcher toward a ship around the time of her disappearance. A small bribe to a dock-worker had revealed that the ship was bound for Alexandria. One of the thespian assassins had taken a ship there to follow up.

Ardeshir had begun to experiment with his own disguises and was astonished at how different people treated him depending on his appearance. He'd always assumed that his skin color was the defining marker by which people responded to him, but it now appeared to him that his social status was an even bigger influence. When he dressed and walked confidently as a trader or vendor, it seemed that slaves, sailors, and shoppers made way for him. When he appeared as a legionnaire, it was like the great sea dividing for Moses. When he donned a faded tunic or robe of a house slave, few gave him any notice at all.

A week into hiding, Tertullian arrived at the warehouse wearing his legion-naire uniform.

"Prince, I've got news for you," he said. "We've learned that after being wounded in the attack at the governor's mansion, your aunt's guardians took her back to Persia. If you want to see her, you'll have to hitch up with the next caravan. We'll keep looking for your father, but I don't think there's much chance he made it to Alexandria."

Tertullian doffed his uniform and slipped into the role of an old man.

"Put on the house slave robe," the man instructed. "I'll be the blind man whom you lead through the market. We have one more visit to make before you leave Caesarea."

As they walked back out into the city, Ardeshir made the argument that he should travel to Alexandria alone to continue the search for his father. This didn't go well with Tertullian, and he suspected it would be no different with the other thespian assassins.

They soon came to a booth in the middle of the market. One of the assassins had been posing as a baker here in order to pass secret messages through the loaves of bread he gave to other members of the network. He had been carefully selecting small loaves and placing them in a woven basket.

"You distract us from our work while you're here," the assassin complained to Ardeshir while he went about his work. "You will be seen for who you are in moments. Your body will end up at the bottom of the sea with your father. Return to Persia and rule your people with wisdom." He handed over a filled basket to the would-be prince. "Then maybe your people and ours can end this centuries-old war that keeps us apart and prevents the silk from flowing freely."

As Ardeshir and Tertullian turned to go, Mariam walked by with a basket filled with market vegetables. She looked at him briefly and Ardeshir's blood quickened in his veins. Had she recognized him?

At first she turned away... but a moment later she came back and tugged on his arm.

"You don't fool me," the woman said. "All those stories about Persia and the emperor's palace? Now I see you for who you are. A street beggar." She backed away. "And to think I thought you would come back to marry me. You're the last man who'll ever play the fool with my heart."

With that, Mariam fled into the crowd.

"I see you've had a little fun during your visit," Tertullian said with a smirk as they watched her go. "What would the queen think if she knew her nephew was playing with the alley maidens?"

"It's not like that," Ardeshir said. "I needed a place to hide and she and her mother took me in. There was never anything between us. She harbored childish fantasies."

Tertullian kept his voice low. "I may pretend to be blind, but even I could see that she was no child. With the right dress and a bit of bathing, that woman could be a queen in her own right. She has the dignity, heart, and fierceness of one who knows what she wants."

Ardeshir tried to find Marian in the crowd, to steal one final glimpse. But no, she was gone. The pang of disappointment was like a knife to his heart.

He turned away. "I need to get back to Persia."

The return trip was as rough and as uncomfortable as the ride out had been. Ardeshir's carriage bounced along with a group of Roman troops who took him to the border of Armenia. From there, six Parthians from the Magi's militia escorted him back to Susa. That wasn't the end of his journey, for a caravan of Arab camel traders then transported him up to the queen's palace in Dar. By the time he reached his final destination, seven weeks had passed and it seemed a lifetime.

All the way, he had distracted himself with three daydreams—Princess Lu Hou, playing the bone flute in the emperor's garden; Farzana, sitting by the fire and rubbing her fingers gently over the lapis lazuli; and Mariam, pouring water into a gourd and handing it to him while staring shamelessly into his eyes.

This latest trip had only led to more complications. Now there were three women who had touched his heart, none of whom could be touched in return.

At the palace in Dar, Ardeshir accepted the chance to bathe in a warm tub and take up a scented robe to cover himself. He felt like a thespian assassin putting on a new persona. As he passed the courtiers, guardians, and militia standing erect at their posts, it seemed as if everyone had taken on a role for this season. It felt as though he was part of a game.

When he entered the throne room, his aged aunt sat limply on the dais with the elegantly gowned servants all around. She raised her head and gestured with a limp wave for him to come forward.

He bowed on one knee and stayed there until he heard her whisper.

"Come, sit with me."

As he sat, her sadness fell over him like a thick cloud.

"Your father is lost to us. My brother is gone." Tears rolled from her eyes and she made no effort to stop them from dropping off her chin and onto her gown. "I am too old to play this role. It is my time to join him. He has explained the way of Yeshua and now I know that the Way is the way. I'm releasing your sister to join you for the trip to the emperor's palace, to bring those horses you promised. Whatever you bring back will form the basis of treasure with which you build this kingdom. These men around us will train you to rule. The Magi will have the ultimate authority, but they'll allow you to live in luxury as long as you follow their desires for you."

The ensuing silence seemed unending. She hung her head to her chest and breathed slowly, as though willing herself to die right there.

A courtier stepped into the room and approached the throne. As he knelt, the queen raised her eyes and shared an unspoken message with nothing but a glance. The courtier nodded, rose, and left her presence.

Moments later, he returned with Yas.

Ardeshir stepped off the dais and rushed to his sister. She was gaunt and haggard but had been washed and fitted with a fine gown. The fire in her eyes was gone, though, the bounce lost in her step. The spirit that had been so prone to laugh and seize joy had evaporated.

Yas hung her head. "I thought you would never return. Take me to the farm. Let me die."

He took his sister by the elbow and drew her toward the throne. From her seat, his aunt looked up.

Ardeshir took a deep breath. "I will return my sister to the farm until she's strong enough for our journey. Then I'll send for the thousand horses. Aunt, you must remain in control until my return."

At her nod, he turned and escorted Yas out of the royal palace. They made their way to the stables, although he deducted that she wasn't ready for a long journey. Still, the two of them needed to create a little space for themselves. Eventually they would be ensconced in this palace, their lives shackled in ways neither of them could presently imagine.

With shame, he realized that in all his fantasies he hadn't pictured the pain that his sister and aunt were enduring while he dreamed of the three other women in his life.

Once they'd gotten underway, Ardeshir spared a glance to look back toward the simple carriage on which Yas was able to lie on a thick bed of sheepskins. They had left the palace before dusk and only now were stopping at the first inn, an hour from the palace.

The main rooms were full, but their host ushered them to a small cabin a short walk into the forest. The three-room brick-and-tile enclosure was snug and filled with handwoven carpets, four clay lamps, and a diversity of hand-carved figurines.

"Who's the craftsman?" Ardeshir asked, fingering the tiny pieces of art.

The innkeeper picked up a well-proportioned camel. "It's my hobby during the low times. If you see anything you like, it's yours. For a reasonable price, of course." He set the piece down and adjusted a blanket at the foot of a reed pallet. "If you need extra blankets, let us know. My wife will be by with your meals soon. It looks like you've been on quite a trip today."

Yas collapsed onto a cushioned chair. "It's been a long day and a long year."

"We'll let you know if we need anything else," Ardeshir assured the man.

"I hope you and your wife enjoy the stay." Their host closed the door.

Ardeshir used a clay lamp to light the fire and warmed his hands by the blaze. "I guess I should have told him we're not married," he said. "Of course, that could have caused more scandal. Even though we're family, I guess we could still marry."

Yas joined him by the fire, extending her palms toward the flames. "I've given up on marriage. I'm too headstrong and don't want any man telling me what to do. You already have someone waiting for you, though, and I wouldn't dare stand in her way."

"Are you talking about the princess?"

She nudged him with her elbow. "Who else might there be?"

The knock on the door kept him from having to answer. The woman of the inn laid out a feast before them, one that was lavish enough that it reminded him of a wedding feast.

"Try this," she said. "It includes pomegranates, walnuts, duck, onions, saffron, cinnamon, and some family spices."

The meal proved to be the food of angels.

When Yas struggled to get up the next morning, they extended their stay one day. In the meantime, their hostess shared another of her recipes.

"This meal has turmeric, lemon juice, eggplant, onions, lamb, and seasonings on rice," the woman said the following evening when she brought their trays.

"I would like to make you the official cook of the realm," Ardeshir said.

The innkeeper's wife smiled. "Oh, that you were someone who could give us hope! The high and mighty in their palaces have no idea how hard it is to live through a day. All I can say is that if you do ever become someone important, don't forget those of us who struggle to get by."

The trip to the farm took two days, allowing for one more stop at an inn not half as welcoming. When they arrived home, Sanjay was weeding in the gardens by the gate. The servant was quick to jump for joy and race to share the latest news. Farzana stood at the entrance to the main hall with a small bundle in her hands. The two cataphracts near the barn waved and wandered over.

Yas stopped briefly to touch the baby's cheek and then stumbled in to find a place to rest.

The staff debriefed Ardeshir on the news, after which he left to stable the horses. Sanjay fell into step with him as he stretched his legs around the property.

"Sir," he said. "Prince, I mean… we have welcomed fifteen more orphans and two widows. We built four new shelters to house them." He pointed toward a group of cabins along the north fence. "Behind them we have built a new pond with koi so you can remember the good aspects of your trip to the emperor's palace. We have a herd of sheep which some of the boys have taken out to pasture. A woman has been teaching the children about poetry and beauty and peace and truth."

The young man had grown in confidence and fluency, and his newfound passion was unleashed through his words.

"We remember that you will be taking a thousand horses to the emperor," Sanjay added as he looked toward an empty field nearby. "We are planning to build a fence around that flat land. The horses may be kept there until we're ready to go."

"Until *we* are ready to go?" Ardeshir asked with a smile. "I see you're becoming quite invested in the farm's fortunes."

Sanjay nodded in deference. "Of course I will accompany you, if you agree. I've had two of the cataphracts train myself and some of the young men to ride so we can work with you to manage the herd. It will be a long trip and you will need many helpers."

"That is true. Thank you for thinking ahead. For now, we have time. The queen will send the horses, and we won't leave until the spring. Until then, I grant you the power to build these fences, train the boys, and gather supplies for our journey."

Ardeshir stopped by the koi pond along his wanderings but failed to see any movement in the waters.

"I don't see any fish," he remarked.

"Not yet," Sanjay said. "We will bring them back from the Han emperor. Did you see my son?"

"Have you accepted Farzana's son as your own then?"

"We have accepted your blessing to live as one. This boy is the child of our heart."

Ardeshir nodded. "Very well. At least one woman in my life will be happy."

Fourteen

The messenger galloped through the farm's gate while the sun maintained its high perch in the sky. Ardeshir recognized him as one of the famous couriers who carried Aramaic transcripts of great importance from one end of the Roman Empire to the other.

A message could travel along the Royal Road from Ephesus to Susa in just seven days, as opposed to the three months that would otherwise have been typical. A series of relay stations and fresh riders kept these messages moving.

Ardeshir's stomach churned at the sight of the messenger. Could the man be carrying news of his father at last?

"News from the east," the messenger called to him.

From the east? Ardeshir knew the postal system stretched all the way to Hindustan, but of course he knew no one in that distant land. Perhaps the message had come from a trader who hoped to make a deal with the Persians.

This thought kept him in place as Sanjay stepped up to receive the message from the rider.

When the courier had galloped away, Sanjay held up the post for his attention.

"Take it inside," Ardeshir called. "I'll look at it later. It's probably for my father."

As the sun touched the western horizon, Ardeshir traipsed into the hall, tired but satisfied that he had marked out the necessary boundaries for the horse pens. Sanjay had grown into a capable young man and took orders well. He also spoke incessantly about his newborn son, his new wife, and his plans and dreams for the farm. Talking with the man felt like being a visitor in his own home.

Yas sat by the fire warming her hands while Farzana and another girl prepared a meal. The baby kicked happily on a sheepskin by Yas's feet, gurgling and smiling with little bubbles forming at the corner of his mouth.

Kneeling beside the boy, Ardeshir tried to imagine a son of his own. With Farzana, the boy would be of darker skin and bigger build. With Mariam, he would be bright-eyed, tall, and full of laughter. With the princess, though? No, he couldn't imagine such a child.

Now, with all three women out of the equation, he considered that it might be time to look for a new option. While Yas would do, the combination wouldn't work well in the long run. Her desire was for horses, battle, and change more so than home, marriage, and children.

A hollow feeling filled his gut as he washed and prepared for the meal. The atmosphere of his home contained much laughter and pleasure, but something was still missing.

"Do you want your message?" Farzana asked after the meal. "Sanjay left it for you."

"It's probably for my father," he mused. "Yas, why don't you open it?"

"What's the point?" she said. "I can't read the Han emperor's language."

"How do you know it's from the emperor?"

"The scroll contains those characters they use. It's probably about the horses. I think they're wondering when we're going to fulfill our promise. I'd hate to wait too long and have him send an army after us. They have ruthless warriors—"

"I don't know how he would expect me to understand what he wants," Ardeshir said. "I've forgotten half of what I learned during my time there. But bring it to me and I'll see how much I can figure out. We might have to find a translator."

"I know a translator in Susa," Farzana spoke up. "I can bring him if it will assist you."

Ardeshir nodded. "Yes! Let's wait and get someone who knows these things. There's no point in frustrating ourselves by guessing on what the emperor wants."

"I'll send Sanjay in the morning," Farzana said.

"Isn't that my job?" Ardeshir asked.

Farzana blushed and bowed her head. "Many pardons, my lord. While you were gone, I have developed habits which are hard to change."

"Be at peace, my friend," Ardeshir said. "This is your home and you are free within it. We will both send Sanjay to fetch the interpreter. Where is your husband staying?"

Again, Farzana blushed. "He has often joined me in the house, but he is also building a cabin for us near the koi pond. We will both stay there with the baby when it's done."

"You are blessed in your plans." Ardeshir smiled. "We are a family on this farm and we help each other. I'll let you send Sanjay to ride into Susa in the morning."

It took two days before the translator arrived back at the farm. The man sported a long silver mustache, red silk cap, and dragon-emblazoned jacket and trousers.

"Many pardons, my prince," said the translator. "I have many messages to translate through the post now that the Silk Road and Royal Road have found each other. The horsemen ride endlessly from one end of our world to the other."

Ardeshir retrieved the scroll and handed it to the translator, who unfurled the hemp paper and laid it out on a table.

"Ah, this is a very important message," the man remarked, studying the characters. "It is intended for the master of the house, the finder of the bone flute."

Fully attentive, Ardeshir leaned over the scroll, trying to fathom the meaning of the foreign characters. "What does it say?"

"There are two messages in one," the translator said. "The first message says, 'Bring the thousand.' The second says, 'Heed the gazebo's call.'"

The translator released the scroll and allowed it to roll up on itself.

"The introduction calls for the speaker of truth to find himself and the thing he has lost," he added from memory. "I'm not sure what that means, but it's for the ears of the receiver to know and understand."

Once the translator had been generously compensated for his trouble, Ardeshir pored over the scroll again and again. The message confused his heart, baffled his mind, and stimulated hope in his soul. It clearly had been sent by the princess; she seemed to be calling him to hurry back. The focus on the thousand was a clear reference to the horses Yas had promised. Perhaps they were needed for some military campaign. As for the mention of the gazebo's call, that was more troubling. And what was this *thing* he had supposedly lost?

Ardeshir had rehearsed the memory of his encounter with the princess at the gazebo hundreds of times in his dreams… the march through the garden hedges, flowers, and fountains until he reached the heights of the palace grounds. The gazebo had been neatly hidden under the hanging vines, with trees all around. The princess had stepped out in a breathtaking costume. He recalled Her flawless Mandarin—"Why must you plague me with questions that grow in my mind?"—and her question about whether he observed her as a man. Their dialogue had confused him that night, but he'd clearly had some effect on her.

And now she was undoubtedly wed to some weak-souled prince who didn't deserve her. Someone who could never bring her the truth of the Way. Surely Liu's relative had to be wrong in saying she was still unwed and waiting.

The hemp paper was getting worn from his constant handling. The ink was beginning to smudge and fade.

Sitting by the fire one evening with Yas and Farzana, Ardeshir sought their counsel. "What do you think the princess means when she advises me to heed the gazebo's call?"

"What happened at the gazebo?" Yas asked.

"She sent me a message to come, so I went. She asked me whether I observed her like a man, because her servant had told her that I did." He paused, weighing how much more to say. "She was going to feed her servant to a leopard if she was wrong, so of course I told her that the servant was right. Then the princess asked me why I plagued her thoughts?"

He fed another log into the fire and waited for it to catch. The others waited.

"I asked her to forgive me and she asked what that meant and what needed to be forgiven," he continued. "I tried to explain how confused I was over everything that had happened between us. Finally, she said that she wanted to give her heart to a man of truth, someone who could bring life. Apparently I was not acting like such a man."

"And were you acting like a man of truth who brings life?" Yas probed.

Ardeshir rose and paced the floor in front of the fire. "Of course I wasn't. You saw what she did to me over the koi pond. She made my mind crazy." He dropped the crumpled message on a counter. "I left with you and now she's telling me to come back and bring the thing I've stolen. What is this thing? If I go back, Yas, you know that the only outcome will involve the general and his leopard."

Yas stood with him and placed her hand on his arm. "Ardie, you're not the same man who stumbled out to the emperor's garden. You're solid now. You know truth… and you know the Way." She moved to the counter and savored a date while holding out a tray to him. "Maybe the thing you've stolen is her heart and she wants you to bring it back."

Ardeshir stopped, hand halfway to the tray. "What do you mean, her heart? She's married to some warrior prince and locked up in a palace somewhere. How in the world could I have stolen her heart? She spent half our time together trying to destroy me."

"Maybe she was trying to find out what kind of a man you are," Yas said. "A man's character is often exposed for what it is in the middle of a challenge. Maybe she was testing you, finding out what kind of heart you had. The closer she got to you, maybe she realized she was losing her heart…"

Ardeshir flopped onto a stool and rested his chin on his knuckles. "You may be a woman, but I don't think you understand the princess at all. The last thing I want to do is take those horses back to the emperor and find out that she has some new torture planned to pay me back for stealing something. For all I know, someone took her bone flute and she thinks it must be me."

Farzana rose to attend to the baby, who cried for feeding.

"Master… prince… you know how I treasured your time and attention before the soldier had his way with me," the new mother said as she nursed her baby. "Until that moment, I had given my heart only to you and felt that I couldn't live if you despised me. You took me into your home! But now I realize that Sanjay is the one my heart belongs to." She stroked the little one's cheek. "Perhaps the princess has been wooed by others but still feels like her heart has been taken by you. Perhaps it's not torture she desires to share but love."

"What do either of you know about true love?" Ardeshir asked. "The world around the emperor's garden isn't like the real world. They have wild animals kept for sport—to hunt and kill. They even hunt their own people! They allow no independence. And if the truth you claim to offer doesn't bear up to their intense scrutiny, you won't last a day."

He reached for his cape and wrapped it around his shoulders on the way to the door.

"How do you women pretend to understand the outside world?" he demanded. "Even if the princess believed she loved me, how would she expect someone like me to survive in a world like that?"

Yas followed him to the door. "Maybe you should be asking yourself how a princess like that might hope to survive in a world like ours."

Fifteen

"How many of these horses do you think will survive the trip?" Ardeshir asked as he and Yas rode among the thousand and ten majestic animals milling about in their large field. "With the spring runoff, we'll have to ford streams, survive ambushes, and find enough pasture along the way. We'll need at least a hundred militiamen and dozens of outriders and donkey carts to join our supply caravan. Even that may not be enough."

"You know what they'll be serving at the banquet in your honor, don't you?" Yas replied. "Donkey for sure. Dog, monkey, and snake will probably be on the menu. If you prove yourself, maybe they'll put that leopard on a spit and roast it up."

"If we make it there with all these horses, I think I'll ask them to roast the elephant!"

It was good to hear Yas chuckle again. Her spirits were back after all that dismal time in the dungeon. Her seething anger toward the queen kept boiling over, but she had softened some and could often be seen in the evenings sitting by the fire playing with Farzana's son.

Ardeshir still hadn't heard any news regarding what had happened to his father, though, and he quietly mourned the loss. He felt the weight of carrying on the farm's legacy while still tossing and turning about his own future. One day he would have to take the throne.

Not helping matters was all the uncertainty of the upcoming journey. He didn't know what life had in store for him.

A few mornings before their departure, he carried a bag out to Yas as she paced around the koi pond.

"Do you remember when we raided the Temple of Fire to rescue you?" he asked.

"If I ever stop remembering, I'm sure you'll remind me. What about it?"

He held out a bag. "This is for you. We took it from the mercenaries guarding the place. I think we can use it to call each other if we ever get in trouble."

She pulled out a pink conch shell. "What do I do with this?"

He gently took it out of her hands and held it to his lips. A long mournful cry echoed through the farm, causing everyone to stop and look in his direction. Even the horses stopped to look.

"How did you learn to do that?" she asked.

"Practice. Now take it and learn. We may need it on the trail."

She smiled. "You'll probably need it more than me, and you already know how to use it. But I'll store it in my pack. Thanks for thinking of me."

A lone rider near the horse pens turned in their direction and charged up the hill.

"Friend, master, prince," Sanjay called from the back of his mount. "That stallion by the fence is creating trouble. We'll end up with many injured horses if we don't restrain it."

Ardeshir looked off toward the pasture just as the implicated Friesian chased down a young, white stallion and nipped at its shoulder. There was little room for the smaller beast to escape, with the fence confining them in every direction.

"For now, I guess it would be better to build a special pen to confine that one," Ardeshir said, noting a spot on the white stallion's shoulder where it had been bitten. "And I'll keep it tied to a cart while we travel. Maybe the emperor, or maybe the general, would appreciate its spirit. In the meantime, get him isolated."

As though for the first time, Ardeshir noticed the large number of white horses milling through the pasture.

"Why have we got so many of these white horses?" Ardeshir asked.

"Those are the Han Xue Ma," Yas replied. "When they run, they almost shimmer. Their blood runs near the surface of their skin and sweats out from their shoulders and neck. I think it's really just that their hair gets darker. Anyway, these are the emperor's favorite warhorses. He'll pay many hundreds of bolts of silk for them. The other horses are Arabian and will also fetch a good price.

"Why does the emperor like the Han Xue Ma so much?" Ardeshir continued, still not satisfied. "I do remember seeing a few of them near the emperor's garden, but I didn't pay attention as to where he got them."

"These are the fastest horses," Yas said. "They can travel a long time with only one drink of water per day. They're perfect for a long trek like this one. I think the emperor will want to breed them so he never again need depend on foreign traders to carry his silk."

Ardeshir let out a whistle. "Maybe we should keep a few of them for ourselves... the princess in her red gown would look magnificent on that white mare..."

Yas elbowed him gently. "But which one of the two are you going to have to tame first?"

The cataphracts slowly returned to the land around the farm after their spring campaigns to the west and south. Bandits and the smaller militias of city monarchs often stretched their reach of authority in this way and the larger power brokers had to then put them in their place. The Magi's militia, working for the queen, had now been consolidated with Ardeshir's cataphracts, forming an uneasy truce. The Magi controlled the northern two-thirds of the Persian Empire as well as a small stretch down to the ocean. Caravans ran freely along clearly defined paths and paid tribute to whoever controlled the right of way.

The priests at Susa had recruited a band of warrior-guardians to promote the cause of Zoroastrianism in the region, which lay in neutral territory between the control of the Magi and the cataphracts.

One of the cataphracts rode to the farm to alert Ardeshir that the Temple of Fire had been pushing the limits of tolerance.

"Prince, I think we may not be finished with our campaigns," he said. "Two young women and a boy were thrown alive into the temple's eternal flame. Surely you can't endorse such a thing. I didn't share your father's faith, but I know he wouldn't tolerate such an act."

"Ready fifty riders," Ardeshir said. "I'll send my sister to lead you."

"Why not lead us yourself?" the rider asked. "If you are to be our prince, you should show your strength in leadership."

The rush of adrenaline Ardeshir felt surprised him. Normally the clash of battle was something Yas yearned for, not him.

"We will attack at dusk when the next flame is stoked," he said. "Choose and prepare the fighters."

Sanjay prepared his warhorse without hesitation. The coat of mail that soon covered the animal unleashed its hidden energy; it stamped restlessly, knowing what was ahead. Ardeshir's own vest matched the beast's mail, making them appear as one in the light of the setting sun.

When he reached the gate, he was met by Yas javelin in hand.

"What is this news I hear?" she asked. "That you will lead the raiding party on the Temple of Fire? Don't you remember who was imprisoned in that place? I should be the one to harvest vengeance on those priests and priestesses."

"We will ride together," Ardeshir said. "It will give me a chance to prove whether your training has been strong enough to prepare me for the journey ahead. Besides, you don't know their tactics. I only want you in this battle if the fire within you won't let you do otherwise."

He turned his steed ahead of the band of warriors that had assembled.

"Take half the men and attack the temple grounds near the oval pool and white mansion where you were held captive," he ordered, finally deciding to let her accompany them. "I will ride with the rest of the men through the front gates. We'll face many enemy forces before we can get close, so we'll need to circle in from the most unexpected approach."

Ardeshir lifted his hand to alert the men, pointing at a group on the fringe.

"You seven men, disguise yourselves as ordinary traders and spy out the land. Gather your intelligence slowly. But once you see your opening, signal so we can strike quickly and fiercely."

Yas leaned in. "Since when did you become the strategist?"

"It's something I learned from the thespian-assassins in Caesarea," he said. "May Yeshua guide your hand and guard your heart as you risk your life for what you love."

"And may he do the same for you."

It wasn't the easiest of victories for the cataphracts. The combined mercenaries from Gaul, Britannia, Egypt, and Ethiopia had prepared an impressive assault for them, with hidden pits, archers, and barriers to thwart Ardeshir's efforts. The eternal flame was stoked high under a full moon in order to allow the priests to track his men's movements. Once the assault had begun, a dozen horses fell into spiked pits camouflaged under reed mats covered with loose grass and branches. Arrows bounced off horse and rider alike; only a few found their mark through the gaps in the armor.

The temple warriors who had hidden in the back half of the property responded to the conch call of the gatekeepers and unveiled themselves before Yas launched her own assault. As the mercenaries moved away from the pool toward the frontal assault, her own men had unleashed a devastating crossbow attack, killing dozens.

The few who remained hidden sounded an alarm from the inside of the white building and the troops soon recognized that they'd been caught in a pincer. A good number ran from the ambush, escaping through the woods on either side of the temple. One of the cataphracts wrapped his javelin in the cape of a dead priest, lit it on fire, and hurled it into the thatched roof of the residence housing the priestesses. The women rushed out screaming; the panic only increased when the roof caved in before all could escape.

"Smash the ring of the eternal flame," Ardeshir yelled in the aftermath. "There will be no more sacrifices in this place."

Two priests threw themselves into the flame, calling on their god to preserve the holy site. Ardeshir's men used javelins to pull the wood and embers out and push them toward the outside arches where the flames licked hungrily at the pillars. As the temple consumed itself, demonic screams shattered the night. Not even the leopard's snarl had been so terrifying.

They buried the dead in the morning, choosing a site beyond the koi pond, and pondered the sacrifice of those who had fought so hard. Was it worthwhile to deprive families of their men so Ardeshir could trumpet his own control over the land?

"Is this what Father would want for us?" he asked Yas as they walked slowly back to the main hall. "He came to this land to discover who he was… and to share the faith of Yeshua. What have we done to follow the path he laid out for us? What are we accomplishing by taking horses to the emperor and fighting these meaningless battles?"

Yas looked out over the thousand horses milling about, trampling the grass. The lone stallion trotted back and forth along the fence, calling for the attention of the herd.

"I think we should have thought of these questions before the queen gathered all these horses for you," his sister said. "It's a little late to turn them loose and pretend we can live in our own little world. The Han emperor may not need these beasts to destroy us with the power already at his disposal."

Sanjay appeared around the corner of the barn. Ardeshir waited as the young man jogged toward him.

"Master, prince, friend… it is decided. I will go with you on this journey."

Ardeshir grasped Sanjay by the forearm and smiled. "Sanjay, you have become my best worker on the farm. You know everything better than I do. I would love for you to join us, but your wife needs you, your son needs you, and others on this farm need you. Please consider being my representative at home while I'm gone."

Sanjay's smile faded and his brows furrowed. At last he nodded.

"I will make this farm the best in all the land," he said as his smile returned. "You will be proud when you come back. Maybe I'll gather another thousand horses so you can keep the emperor happy."

Yas chuckled. "Sanjay, the only person my brother wants to make happy is the emperor's daughter. You take care of the people here and we'll take care of the horses there."

Farzana stepped out of the main house and moved toward them, babe in arms.

"Whether we go or stay, the next generation will come and go," Yas observed. "Perhaps these horses are a chance given to you by Yeshua to open a door to share the Way. There is still much to live for, even if the princess won't forgive you for stealing her heart."

Ardeshir elbowed Yas and knocked her off-stride. "Promise me you won't bring that up again on the journey," he said. "I may have to send you back on your own."

Yas chuckled. "I'd like to see you try. You may overpower a few poorly trained mercenaries, but I'm not about to fall to your efforts so easily."

She broke off from the walk to stop and take the baby in her arms.

"Too bad this one wasn't a little older," she called over her shoulder. "I would give up my horse and javelin and settle for a few of my own."

The horses moved surprisingly easily over the rough terrain of the mountain passes, and the rogue stallion refrained from straining on its ropes after the first two weeks of being harnessed to a cart.

By the time they were navigating the road toward Hindustan, one horse had been bumped over the edge of a narrow trail and broken its leg. It had been put out of its misery. Another had panicked at a snake and snarled itself in vines, also breaking a leg.

The supply of ten spare horses dwindled as they fought streams and survived two ambushes.

Despite the warmth of the lower plains, the snowy terrain challenged the herd. The men responsible for corralling the beasts had little chance on narrow ledges and had to trust the horses to press on with sure-footed determination.

Twice, at the end of a snowy crossing, dozens of horses broke free from their supervision to charge across a grassy plain before being chased down and returned. On one occasion, a horse escaped and could not be caught; they let it go.

They stopped at a familiar rocky outcropping which offered a dazzling view of the highest peaks in the world. Ardeshir knew this marked the halfway point of their journey. They had one month still to go.

"Remember this place?" Yas asked. "I told you this was your last chance to turn back toward the princess. Somehow you've survived ambushes, the loss of our father, and attacks on the farm. I didn't think you'd get a second chance to go back."

"I won't ask what you mean," Ardeshir said. "And I still don't know if I failed our father on that trade mission, nor do I know what awaits me there. Maybe the leopard made a snack of whatever man the princess ended up marrying."

Yas spat on the ground at his feet. "May the Almighty forgive your tongue for that wish."

Ardeshir unstrapped his gourd and knelt by a stream to refill it with fresh water. "My very survival depended on my tongue last time I was in the emperor's garden. Now I can't think of a single truth that would be strong enough to spare my life. I better start remembering some of the things Father used to teach."

Just then, a cataphract rode up and waited for his attention.

"Prince, the men are tired and the way has been harder than we realized," the man reported. "These horses need time to fill themselves and regain their strength. They're growing thinner and weaker, and I fear they're in no shape for the last push."

The plain below had a bending river that would provide a natural barrier for the herd. There was plenty of lush grass and enough room for the horses to spread out.

"Stake the rogue stallion to a fixed tether and post a rotating guard along the trail to keep the horses contained," Ardeshir ordered. "We will take a week to rest. You may organize the sentries. This is the last place I would want any surprise or ambush."

As the warrior rode away, Yas swung down off her horse and wobbled to a rock where she sat.

"If anyone doubted who's in charge of this expedition, they don't need to wonder anymore," she said. "I haven't had a soldier approach me for the last month. You are confident, clear, and concise. But I'm here should you ever need a break."

Ardeshir joined her and sat on the rock beside her, gazing at the horses as his men herded them down onto the plain. "When we get to the emperor's palace, they will remember you, not me. I'll need you to be as strong as you were the last time. You and I know that something is different… but they won't know. And they may not respond well if I mishandle my authority."

Yas stood up and stretched. "I'll be the first to take out the leopard and general, if only you'll give that princess back her heart and show her who you really are. If you don't disappoint me, I won't disappoint you."

Sixteen

A contingent of more than a hundred red-vested guardians met the caravan a few days outside of the emperor's palace. Ardeshir attempted to
greet them in Mandarin.

"Good morning. How are you? I am Ardeshir. This is my sister Yas."

The rapid reply overwhelmed him as he scrambled to translate. All he could
make out was "Thank you."

As the guardians spread out to escort them, Yas rode close to her brother.
"What did you say?"

"I have to be careful," Ardeshir said. "The language of the Han has thousands
of different pen strokes per word. Each of those words, although they may look
alike, then means different things depending on which of five different tones one
uses. For example, the characters for *horse* could also mean *mother* or numb or
to scold."

"Sounds confusing. No wonder you had trouble communicating with the
princess. In Persia, you could write a love poem and everything would be solved.
Here, you might say the wrong thing completely and not even know it."

Ardeshir cringed. "I'd know it. She'd feed me to the leopard without a second
thought. It's best to keep my mouth shut and hope she finds a way to tell me
what she wants."

"Maybe that gardener friend of yours can translate. Keep you out of trouble." Yas's attention was stolen by the leader of the guardians, who was nodding
in their direction. "That lead guardian is nodding at us. I think he wants to talk
some more. Listen hard."

When they approached, one of the guardian's men stepped forward to provide a rough translation.

"He wants to know who the horses are for," the translator said to Ardeshir.

"The emperor."

"How many are for the emperor?"

"All of them. Although perhaps fifty horses could be spared for the guardians."

The translator shared the message, then turned back. "We will only take the weakest, thinnest, ugliest ones."

Was he kidding? It didn't sound like a joke. Was this a demand for payment in exchange for escorting them? Ardeshir realized he should have brought more of the horses.

"We can discuss this with the emperor," Ardeshir said. "They are his horses."

The leader of the guardians smiled and turned his horse away without another word.

"You negotiate well for a Persian," remarked the translator. "Maybe you will also convince the emperor to give you a good price for these animals."

Ardeshir nodded, turned his mount, and fell back in line with Yas.

"How many was he hoping for?" Yas asked.

"Fifty."

"Were you imagining the leopard when you said no?"

"I didn't say no," Ardeshir said. "I told him these were the emperor's horses and we could talk it over with him."

"Maybe you'll survive here after all."

The guardians pointed toward a large paddock a short distance from the first hedges that marked the entrance to the road leading to the emperor's palace. Yas turned back to help the cataphracts and riders move the animals into place, counting them as they trotted by. One thousand and one of the horses had survived the journey.

"Wait!" the translator told Ardeshir. "Stop here. We'll tell you when you are wanted."

It was three days before the leader of the guardians returned with any news. Ardeshir's heart leapt at the sight of Liu running behind him. But there was no sign of the general or the princess.

The translator soon appeared again. "That running man is the emperor's horse man. He will choose the best horse to demonstrate their quality. He will also determine the price in silk and jade for what you have brought in trade."

Ardeshir nodded and dismounted.

To his surprise, Liu jogged past him without acknowledgement and went straight to the horses. Walking slowly among the herd, the former gardener ran his hands over the animals' flanks, necks, and muzzles before returning to the rogue stallion that had been tied to a fencepost.

"This one," Liu said to the leader. "Take this one to the emperor. It has fire in its heart."

As the lead guardian led the stallion behind his own mount back toward the palace, Liu jogged back down the road without a look or a word. His job was done.

Yas rode up to her brother. "Wasn't that the gardener you made friends with?"

"Yes, it was. He didn't even look at me. Have I changed so much that he didn't recognize me?"

"Maybe your beard is longer. You ride more confidently. You're wearing an armored vest, and you're carrying a javelin." She looked over the rest of the riders. "I guess maybe you blend in with the rest of us? He probably didn't expect you. Or maybe the princess told him not to have anything to do with you."

"I'm going to find him and talk to him myself," Ardeshir said.

He mounted his horse and trotted toward the palace. As he moved, a solid wall of guardians formed across his path, their crossbows notched.

Halting, he waited as the guardians walked toward him, unwavering in their aim.

"Wuh jeow Ardeshir," he called, fumbling for words. "Friend of the princess."

One of the riders, the translator, broke off and approached so that the horses stood neck to neck in opposite directions.

"You cannot enter the emperor's garden. No stranger may come here. It is a sacred place for truth, light, beauty, and hope. Go back."

Confused and disillusioned, Ardeshir turned back. Had he ridden all this way only to find that he wouldn't get a chance to see the princess? He was determined not to let his journey end this way.

But glancing over his shoulder, he noted that the guardians still had their crossbows focused right at him.

It took a week to barter for the appropriate amount of silk and jade they expected in exchange for the horses.

"A bad season for mulberry leaves," the translator claimed. "Not many worms making good silk."

When an inspection of the emperor's stock was made, it seemed to Ardeshir that the silk was sufficient and not at all inferior.

Then came the next excuse: "Horses are lame from travel. Not good like ones up north."

It was clear that this translator didn't have a clear understanding of what constituted a superior horse and what kind of breed the emperor wanted.

When the leader of the emperor's cavalry was called, however, the man was very pleased with the herd. He offered the entire lot, including the stallion, without further delay.

From the moment the last of the horses disappeared down the emperor's road, Ardeshir set in for an anxious wait for the silk and jade. He left the task of watching over the caravan to his sister while he went into the nearby market and probed the stalls for anyone who could convey a message for him into the emperor's garden.

The rows of wooden stalls, neatly ordered under fluttering red canopies, still occupied one side of the dirt path. Fruit vendors still sold peaches, plums, melons, apricots, pears, and other delicacies. On the other side, under white canopies, vendors still sold vegetables like mustard greens, taro, bamboo shoots, beans, millet, rice, and wheat. The brown canopies still housed chickens, fish, rabbits, pigs, dogs, and donkeys, not to mention rodents and birds in cages. The noise provided as much sensory overload as the first time he'd walked these aisles.

He focused his search on the teashop near the far side of the market. When he found it, the façade had changed although it remained part of the same petal around the central fountain. The wiry vendor, with the long white goatee, yellow-tasseled red cap, dragon-emblazoned blue shirt, and red trousers with astrological symbols was nowhere in sight.

A young woman in a blue robe served the tea and pointed him toward an isolated table on the fringe of the establishment.

"I am looking for friend," he opened. "An old man."

"He die," she replied. "He my father. Give self to lions."

Where was the translator when he needed one? "I don't understand. Your father was the old man who owned this teahouse? Is that right?"

"Yes."

"You said he died."

"Yes."

"You said he gave himself to the lions."

"Yes."

"Do you mean he let them eat him?"

"Yes. He old. Time to go."

Spinning around, he took in the other vendors. There were no aged men or women present. What kind of a place was this where the aged served as food for the wild animals?

The tea in front of him had cooled before he took his first sip. The noodles filled his belly, but a deeper emptiness was growing inside.

He called over the teahouse owner's daughter and spoke quietly. "Your father had friends inside the emperor's garden. Do you have the same friends?"

Her eyes enlarged just enough to portray fear. But then she cleared his bowl, porcelain spoon, and chopsticks and took them away.

Minutes later, she returned with a small cookie and slip of hemp paper. On it, in Mandarin, was a simple message: *"Let's go."*

"Follow far," she said as they left the teashop.

Ardeshir palmed the note and slowly rose from his table.

As the woman slipped around a corner of a hedge, he paced himself to follow, trying to appear nonchalant and interested in the plants and birdlife. He rounded the hedge and detected a flash of blue near a bamboo structure some distance ahead. He picked up his pace, scanning the path for anyone who might be watching him. A young boy was the lone candidate to arouse suspicion.

At the bamboo structure, he stopped and leaned back against what seemed like a tool shed. The boy walked up to him and hesitated.

"Go away," Ardeshir said. "I'll feed you to the leopard."

The boy's eyes got big, but he stood his ground. "I take you to where you need to go."

Unsure of whether to trust the boy, Ardeshir finally nodded. "Take me!"

The boy led him into a maze of hedges which seemed to twist and turn in every direction. At one point he spotted the roof of the Red Palace, but the hedges got taller and taller until he couldn't see in any direction, the world reduced to the quickly moving boy and green walls around him. He counted four fountain gardens as they passed through…

Suddenly, he glanced up and realized that the boy had slipped away. He raced forward to look for him but came to a dead end.

He retraced his steps, trying to return to the last fountain garden, but the passage no longer seemed to make any sense.

As shadows filled the pathways, portending the arrival of evening, he heard the distinctive snarl of a leopard in the distance. Ice raced through his veins and made his feet feel like lead anchors.

And then he heard it—the long, mournful cry of the conch sounding somewhere off to his right. Yas had remembered him!

He decided that he must have been moving in the wrong direction. Fighting his instinct, he walked closer to the sound and then tried to scale a hedge to get to its source. If only he could gain some height to view the surrounding landscape and get his bearings…

He tried climbing in three places before managing to wedge his feet onto a sturdy enough branch. As he neared the top of the hedge, which towered twice his height, the branches sank like a soft bed under him. Still, he wrestled his way higher.

Giving in to exhaustion, he lay sprawled on top. As he did, he once again heard that distinctive snarl, followed by the guttural command of General Ban Chao.

"Hunt! Claws, Hunt!"

Just then, Ardeshir's left leg began to slip through the branch, unsettling his balance. He gripped the foliage for dear life and held his breath.

The mournful conch sounded again, this time to the west.

A blanket of darkness slithered across the sky and settled over all he could see. Not a single torch flickered to break the ensuing blackness. Not a single star shone.

The presence, scent, and spirit of the general hovered all around.

"Smell Persian," Ban Chao whispered. "Close."

A branch near Ardeshir's head shook and almost dislodged him.

"Smell fear. Smoke. Horse."

The sound of animalistic panting nearby gave way to horrifying memories of that long ago night when he'd been at the general's mercy. If he ever got hold of that boy who had led him here, there would be no mercy either.

"Nothing here, Claws, nothing here," the general huffed. "Hunt, Claws! Hunt!"

Ardeshir heard a soft scuffing as the hunters moved off, but he hardly dared breathe until they were gone.

Seventeen

The sun had come up well before Ardeshir risked dropping to the path below. The way was littered with the scattered debris of the hedge he'd climbed. If the general had hunted in daylight, it would have given away his presence here.

He moved quickly. The first fountain plaza he encountered had five trails entering and exiting. The cool water provided him an opportunity to wash his face and hands, take a sip of refreshment, and calm his nerves.

Silence had once again settled over the grounds of the emperor's gardens. The sun's path provided the best hope of leading him to freedom, but the problem proved difficult. With the maze curving back and forth, often twisting in on itself, he couldn't ever travel in the direction he hoped to go.

Twice he came across fountains which quenched his thirst and cooled his brow. At the third fountain, though, he pondered the carefully carved characters that appeared in the ceramic bowl. Learning this ancient tongue seemed to be the key to survival.

As he sat down in frustration at the fountain's base, he noticed the image of a dragon that appeared out of sequence with the rest of the mythic motif. Its head pointed toward one of the five trails.

Gaining hope, and in desperation, he took that trail and shortly came to another fountain plaza. An almost identical dragon faced another specific trail. He took that path and this time forced himself into a jog.

Another fountain popped out of the hedges. Once again, the dragon pointed the way.

The direction seemed wrong in light of the sun's journey, but he set his sandaled feet on the path and moved as quickly as he dared.

Suddenly, the hedges ended. He found himself standing behind the market with the same bustle and noise as the day before.

His first temptation was to head to the teashop and unleash his temper on the old vendor's daughter. Fearing unexpected reprisals, however, he determined instead to find Yas and give her an update. Her conch had been a call of distress. They needed to connect as soon as possible.

When he found her standing with the horses at the entrance to the village, she was in a heated exchange with their translator. As he approached her from behind, the translator pointed in his direction and Yas swiveled and stared at her brother with her mouth open.

"Where have you been?" she yelled. "I've been out looking for you all night. They wouldn't let me anywhere near the emperor's garden. If you've been playing games with that princess, or any other woman, I will remove your head right now without a second thought."

He held up his hand and backpedaled, ignoring the smirking translator who turned and walked away.

Yas swung her sword meaningfully above her head, forcing Ardeshir to sink down onto a stump and wait for her to cool.

"What do you think you're doing?" she asked again. "I called you on the conch. You told me that you would come if I used it, no matter what you were doing. The cataphracts thought I had lost my mind to wake everyone up."

He bowed his head onto the heels of his hands. "I was almost eaten by the leopard."

"How did that happen?"

He sighed. "I went to a teashop to see an old friend, but the old man had died. His daughter took me toward the hedges of the emperor's gardens... and then I lost sight of her. A boy told me that he knew the way and I followed him... until he, too, disappeared." Ardeshir craned his neck to get a better look at his sister's eyes. "I ran farther and faster until it was dark, at which point I heard the leopard prowling the maze. I crawled up on top of a hedge as the general passed right beneath me. That's when you blew the conch. I couldn't move! But then they left me."

Yas knelt in front of him and took his hands. "I can't keep saving your life every time we come here. I'm not your mother. Somehow you have to survive on your own." She rose, grabbed a pack, and handed over a small bundle with fruit, cheese, flatbread, and dates. "Eat something. We can't have the leopard thinking all Persians are as thin as their bamboo stalks."

Yas left him with the caravan supplies while she strolled through the market each morning for food. The traders who had accompanied them also continued to barter for items of interest, but the trade mission was clearly coming to an end.

Each afternoon, brother and sister rode the perimeter of the emperor's garden looking for ways to communicate with someone on the inside. Their frustration grew over time. Whenever they came close, the people scattered. Something was amiss.

After the fifth morning, Yas arrived back from the market and set a collection of fruits and vegetables in the back of his cart.

"I met a horse trader at the market today, someone you knew," she said. "He walked by and handed me a small bag. I'm sure it's for you."

She held the woven blue, red, and gold bag out for him.

Inside Ardeshir found three items: a horse carved from mahogany, a porcelain teacup with a blue dragon on it, and a piece of hemp paper. He laid them on a stump and tried to discern their meaning.

The horse was likely to signify Liu.

He raised the porcelain cup, examined the dragon, and looked for hidden characters on the bottom. Nothing. As he sniffed it, the scent of tea grew strong and an image came to him of sharing a meal with Liu's family—on the night the leopard had taken Liu's sister. "Your cup. Your home," Liu had said that night. The cup now seemed to be a reminder of that welcome.

In light of these two items, it didn't make sense that Liu had so far ignored them.

He looked to the hemp paper for understanding. It wasn't a large piece and the writing on it was limited to three words. He wracked his brain to grasp its significance, but it had been too long since he'd immersed himself in Mandarin.

Ardeshir wandered to the market, looking for a sympathetic face. Without fail, every vendor lowered their eyes as he passed.

Volcanic anger surged from his gut and up his chest until he was ready to unleash a torrent of terror on the timid villagers. But what good would it do? They wouldn't understand his Persian dialect any more than he would understand them.

Resting by a fountain, he caught that familiar flash of blue out of the corner of his eye. It was the old man's daughter again, purchasing supplies for her teahouse. Calming the rush of adrenaline he felt, he forced himself to remain still until she had completed her transaction.

He followed her to the teahouse and called to her as she entered the place.

She turned, the panic in her eyes clear. "No, no, no…"

The woman dropped her supplies and backed into a corner with her hands over her head. She sank down and hid her face in her sleeves.

Ardeshir stood over her, waiting. "I don't understand you."

She finally looked up; only her eyes showed. "General say you eat baby. He say run."

He sat at a table, watching as she slowly unraveled herself and stood up with her back to a wall. He picked up her groceries, returned them to their bags, and set them on a counter.

When he returned to his seat, he held out the piece of hemp paper.

"Help," he said.

Eyeing her escape routes, she moved away from the wall. When a customer arrived, she spoke rapidly with him and pointed at Ardeshir, who sat calmly with his hand extended.

The customer then snatched the message and scanned the three words. He spoke quickly to the old man's daughter.

The young woman nodded. "It say, 'Come now gazebo.'"

Yes, the message had to have come from the princess. But why would Liu send it to him? He'd been through this before. If she was married, why was she calling him? And how could he get into the garden? Maybe the general was laying a trap for him.

Ardeshir retrieved the message and raced back through the market to their camp. There, Yas was whittling an elongated piece of thick bamboo, boring holes with her carving knife.

"A blowing pipe," she explained. "I saw them at the market and figured I could make one. Maybe I could use this to call you without waking the whole village."

He extended the paper with the princess's message. "It's from her."

"Who?" Yas set down her bamboo pipe and rose to examine the paper. "The princess? There's no use showing me this. I can't read it." She waved him off with the back of her hand. "How do you know it's not a trap?"

He tucked the message away in his robe pocket. "That's what I've been wondering. No one knows the princess met me secretly in that gazebo. It happened the day before the banquet they held in your honor."

Ardeshir paused to look toward the red-tiled palace in the distance, rising over the far end of the maze of hedges.

"I have to find out a way in," he mused. "The only way to the palace is through the maze, through the fortress of the guardians, or through the park of wild things."

"So what's stopping you?" Yas asked. "I'll go along. We can take some of the cataphracts as well. They're bored and looking for some action."

"Too much action and the emperor will ensure we never leave this place," Ardeshir said. "Pick one or two others and we'll go in through the park tonight. There are lions, tigers, leopards, elephants, snakes, and other beasts that hunt at night. And once we go over the wall, there will be no coming back the way we got in."

Yas grinned widely, an expression he hadn't seen since she had held Farzana's baby.

"You just show us where to go," she said. "The moon is full tonight, so we'll be able to see. Our armored vests might be noisy, but we need all the protection we can get… along with our javelins, daggers, and swords." She raised her arms in a champion's pose. "It's claws and jaws against the Persian warriors. Get yourself ready. We'll meet you behind the market when the sun goes down."

Darkness had wrestled dusk into a stranglehold when Yas found Ardeshir getting ready in his tent. She tapped Ardeshir on the shoulder and chuckled at his jump of surprise.

"Who were you expecting?" she asked. "I told you we'd be here when the sun went down."

"I didn't hear you coming," he said. "There's nothing out here but frogs and crickets. And I was sure all that metal would give you away."

"It takes practice to walk this way. I brought three of the cataphracts. We made a ladder to scale the wall. One of the men will send it over with us so we can use it to get out again."

"Good! You think of everything. The trail we need to find is down the road. We should get in before the moon comes up over the hills."

He glanced outside the tent at the cloudless sky. The giant moon shone brightly.

"One place of entry is as good as another tonight," Yas said. "Let's just get up and over. There's no telling when the guardians might come through and find us. Or the general with his leopard…"

The ladder made scaling the wall easy. A cataphract hoisted the contraption over after the team had climbed onto the path beyond. Then he slipped away.

Ardeshir was only halfway down the ladder when he heard a snarl. Yas was already at the base holding the ladder.

"Hurry!" she whispered.

Once all four explorers had reached the ground, they held the ladder in front of them in a defensive posture.

"There's four of them," Yas said, spotting eyes shining at them through the darkness.

"You mean four eyes or four beasts?" Ardeshir asked. "Let's stay as close to the hedge wall as we can and keep the ladder in front like a shield."

As they moved, the eyes slowly followed them. And from time to time, those eyes disappeared for extended periods. Unnervingly, Ardeshir never knew when they would reappear—but they always did.

All went well, until they arrived at a wide pond which separated them from the edge of a forest on the other side. The moon reflected beautifully on the shimmering surface.

The water was too wide to cross with the ladder. They could skirt around it, but those eyes were waiting for them along the shoreline.

"I guess we have to go around and face the beasts," Yas whispered.

Ardeshir crouched and examined the edge of the pond. "An old carver once spoke to me about some water near a den of lions. I wonder if this is what he was talking about…"

As they crept along the water's edge, watching the forest, they were startled by a thunderous splash and a short scream. Ardeshir pivoted.

One of their men was missing. Before he could fully register what was going on, he saw Yas drop the ladder into the water close to where a hand was straining upward from the depths. Suddenly, the water began to thrash and the hand dipped below the surface.

Only stillness remained as Yas withdrew the ladder.

"Attack behind us!" warned the remaining cataphract.

Ardeshir and Yas turned and found themselves facing four lions advancing toward them in a hunting stance. They roared, seeking to instill fear in their victims, who had nowhere to run.

It worked.

"Hold the ladder out front and point your javelins out," Yas ordered. "And keep an eye on the water!"

The lions appeared to understand their tactics and crept slowly forward, tails flicking in anticipation. Behind the pride, a cackle of hyenas crawled out of the shrubs, laughing hysterically. Even an elephant crashed through a stand of bamboo; it raised its trunk and let out a bellowing trumpet blast, only to stampede away again.

Ardeshir's eyes went wide, trying to grasp the chaos that had been unleashed.

"Back to the hedge wall!" he cried out. "We've got to climb up to safety!"

"I'll go last," Yas volunteered, already backing up.

The cataphract cut her off. "No! It's my duty." He broke into a jog. "Get up as quickly as you can. I'll hold them off as long as I can…"

Ardeshir swung the ladder up against the hedge and clambered up. By now, more of the lions had joined the pack, and he heard them snapping at their flank.

Yas was halfway up behind him when Ardeshir finally turned—just in time to see the cataphract thrust his javelin into the chest of a leaping lion. The man held on tight, but then another lion snatched the weapon with its jaws and heaved him forward. Dropping the broken javelin, the cataphract slashed with his sword in one hand and brandished his dagger in the other.

Yas hurled her javelin into the throat of a lion to buy the man time, then raced up to join Ardeshir atop the wall.

The cataphract climbed as quick as he could, but the pride knocked the ladder over and sent him tumbling. The animals were on him before he had a chance to gain his feet. The fight was over in moments. All Ardeshir could do was watch the beasts tear at his throat.

He turned to his sister and held to her, trying to shut out the bedlam below. It was one thing to die at the hands of another man in battle. But to be torn apart by ruthless animals?

The lions took a few last bites, then lost interest in their prey and prowled off into the forest. The hyenas took advantage of their disregard to rush in and finish the job they'd started. The cackling creatures fought for scraps.

Just then, a long sinuous body broke through the surface of the water and slithered to the base of the wall. Ardeshir swallowed back his terror as the giant snake—an anaconda, he thought—snapped its jaws into the leg of one of the hyenas and dragged the screeching form into the water.

Ardeshir vomited. How close they had come to death. How foolish he had been.

"We need to go," Yas said. "We need to go. If we wait here the rest of the night, we'll have wasted the sacrifice of my men. When the guardians catch us, they'll make sure we're the next meal for those beasts."

"The guardians will find the ladder and know we were here. They'll come looking for us."

"Hopefully they'll find the cataphract's armor and think he was alone."

They crawled atop the wall with great care, moving slowly over the parts of the hedge that seemed most precarious. The path forward was narrow and their fingers gripped whatever branches were strong enough to steady them.

An eternity later, as the moon threatened to drop from the sky, they reached the outer stone wall that surrounded the emperor's garden. A thick branch curled up towards it; if they climbed it, they could probably reach the safety of the wall.

Ardeshir went first, but quickly realized there was a gap between the branch and the wall, one he could only cross by making a jump for it.

"Don't miss," Yas hissed at him. "It's a long way down."

Ardeshir counted slowly to three, then hurled himself forward through the breach. His vest slammed against stone, sounding like a gong in the night. With both arms, he clung to the stone wall, almost losing his grip. His raw fingers fought to gain purchase.

At last he pulled himself up the rest of the way, breathing heavily from terror and exertion.

A moment later, Yas smashed into the wall right behind him. He helped her up, then gave her a minute to recover.

"I've probably lost all the skin off my hands," Yas remarked, shaken. "What now?"

Ardeshir peered into the night. "I think I recognize this place. The wall dips up ahead. We can drop to the ground there… it's only a short walk to the gazebo."

Yaz looked around uncertainly, but there were no beasts or guardians in sight in this part of the garden.

"Are you sure?"

But Ardeshir was already on the move. "Just watch out for snares. Liu once told me the guardians sometimes set traps."

"This place seems so upside-down," she remarked.

"You'd be amazed how many things seem that way here."

"Are you sure this princess is worth the trouble?" Yas asked.

"We'll soon find out. No more talking!"

Eighteen

rdeshir and Yas huddled in the gazebo until the sun rose above the garden. They could hear workers till the soil nearby as the guardians patrolled the paths. Clouds rolled in and a short sprinkle doused the landscape.

"What do we do now?" Yas asked from their hiding place. "Not a soul has even looked this way."

"The princess has a routine," Ardeshir whispered. "She'll be at the koi pond, then go for her meditation and massage and sit for a lesson with whoever her teacher is now. She'll come up here in the afternoon when others take naps."

"What about her husband?" Yas asked. "If she's been married off to a prince from another kingdom, why is she still here at the palace?"

"If I knew what's in a woman's mind, I wouldn't be hiding in this gazebo. Besides, I have no idea when that message was written. It could have been a year ago, for all I know."

Both their stomachs were gurgling by midafternoon. Their lips cracked and their tongues cleaved to the roof of their mouths.

"Should have brought some food or water," Yas said. "Thought we'd be back at the camp by now."

Ardeshir peered through the vines. "Someone's moving in this direction," he said. "I think it's Liu."

The pair sheltered in the gazebo and waited. Sure enough, Liu soon appeared and began raking the grass.

After working for a few minutes, the former gardener raised his head. "Are you here?" he asked in Persian.

Yas looked pointedly to her brother and held her fingers to her lips.

"Are you here today?" Liu asked again. "I heard the lions were fed last night."

Ardeshir stood up and peeked his head through an opening in the vines. "Yes… why have you been avoiding me?"

Liu smiled in relief at the sight of his old friend. "The general asks every day if any of us has met with you. He hopes you'll leave soon… before seeing the princess."

"What do you mean?" Ardeshir asked. "Why is he worried about that?"

"He desires the princess for himself, but she has given her heart to you. She's been awaiting your return."

Ardeshir's mouth fell open in shock. "What happened to her suitors?"

"The general told them that any man worthy of the emperor's daughter would have to survive for three days in this park of wild animals. Only three men agreed to try, and none of them survived. Ban Chao has made his own claim, of course, but the princess delays. He grows restless." Liu looked down to the ground and continued his raking. "He believes the princess will only accept him if he can destroy you."

"And what does the emperor want?" Yas asked.

"The emperor will do what his daughter desires." Liu knelt in the soil, unearthed a few rocks which he piled together, and spoke to his friend. "The princess heard that you came back with the horses and that the emperor was pleased with your gift and the simple price you asked for such fine animals. So she passed me that message and came here to the gazebo every day for a week, hoping to meet you. But I couldn't deliver the message right away. Then the general warned her to stay away, telling her there was a dangerous animal loose in this part of the garden."

"Your Persian is much finer than my Mandarin," Ardeshir remarked.

"There is a slave in the emperor's kitchen who I speak with every day," Liu said. "He's a fine chef and fine teacher. Perhaps you can meet him before you leave again."

But Ardeshir had bigger concerns. "How will I meet the princess if she's staying away?"

"I will pass a note to the chef, who will tell the princess. I hope she comes here after her dinner tonight." Liu blinked. "Are you hungry?"

"More than you know," Yas said. "Can you get us something?"

"Perhaps the princess can bring food." Liu stroked his beard. "How were the lions fed last night?"

"We came through the park… and two of my men were unsuccessful," Yas said. "There must be an easier way into this place."

"If there was, the general would have blocked it by now." Liu turned to Ardeshir. "We pride ourselves in being a world apart, and I don't see any way in which you and the princess can be together. Not while the general controls this place. The guardians are watching the garden so carefully now. There may be no way out."

Without a further word, he grasped his rake and strode down the hill toward the palace.

"I guess we have nothing to do but wait," Yas said to her brother.

Ardeshir continued to peer through the vines until he saw the palace door open and two guardians step out with the princess between them. He gasped upon seeing her beauty. As he watched, the princess fidgeted with the yellow chrysanthemum in her hair and looked in his direction. Did she know he was observing her? He ducked back out of view.

Half an hour later, he heard the faintest crunch of a leaf and then heard the voice he had been longing to hear.

"You may wait below," the princess said to Liu. "I would like privacy in my shelter. Thank you for your good work."

As she stepped into the gazebo, Ardeshir knelt facedown to the ground.

The princess spoke in Persian. "What is wrong with your brother?"

Yas looked up in surprise at having been addressed first. "He is overwhelmed by your beauty. We have come a long way for this moment and he's lost for words."

"Tell him to rise."

"Get up!" Yas said to her brother.

Ardeshir sat back on his haunches as he took in the glory before him. The scent of jasmine was stronger than ever. Her lips were set firm and her eyes bored through him.

"If you see me like a man sees a woman, why do you not respond to my messages?" she asked. "You left without a word. I have waited and thought about the truths you taught, but they do not seem to matter to you. Why are you trying to prove yourself to people who don't matter when you know it won't get you what you want?"

"Your Persian is flawless," he said.

"My chef is Persian and a good teacher. I have had a year to learn."

"Why are you learning Persian?"

She slapped both of her hands against her thighs. "Are you so thick-headed? You cannot understand my language. If we were to talk, I had to learn yours. Why did you take so long to come back?"

He breathed deeply as he fought to sort out his own confused thoughts. "Many things happened while I was away. We had to gather the horses, my father disappeared, and there has been trouble in my kingdom."

"You stole my heart," she said, pacing. "I sent a message telling you to return it, and still you did not come. Many others have come to take it, but I did not have it to give. The general circles me like a hungry leopard waiting to take me for himself. Who will save me?"

"I am sorry. I thought you were taken by another and would not want me to return."

She stomped her foot. "Then why did you come back? Without my heart, I cannot play my flute, cannot dance, and cannot meditate in peace. Return what you have stolen."

Ardeshir stood and backed up against the gazebo wall. "How do I return your heart? I don't understand."

She glared as though with fire. "Tell me now that you care nothing for me as a man cares for a woman. Tell me that you will walk away from this garden and never return. Tell me that you would rather me be with the general than with you."

He bowed his head. "I cannot wish you to any other man."

She reached out for him and took his chin, forcing it up so he could look at her. "Then declare yourself. Fight for me. Woo me. Speak the truth to the emperor and claim my heart forever."

"But I am just a man. An ordinary man. You are a princess. The daughter of the emperor."

She dropped her hand. "You are a prince. You are a warrior. You are a teacher. You are a bringer of a truth that is greater than any truth we have known. Speak it."

"How will I speak it? I cannot meet with the emperor. I have no one to open the way for me."

"You have me." She reached out and took hold of the sleeve of his robe.

"Can my sister join us?" Ardeshir asked.

"Your sister can stay with the chef," the princess said. "I will be all you need."

That next evening's visit to the palace was the strangest Ardeshir had ever experienced. It began with a banquet that proved to be everything Yas had once promised him long ago; they consumed monkey, donkey, snake, dog, fish, squid, and many other unrecognizable dishes. He kept his face down as he skewered each item given to him. He had learned a few novel eating techniques over the years, but his ability to mimic the deft handling of these foods proved limited.

Right after dinner, the emperor led his council of advisors and grand officials, along with Ardeshir, out of the judgment hall and took them into a large, sandy-floored arena. As Ardeshir watched, the emperor climbed onto a dais so high that his visage, once he'd sat on his throne, was beyond reading—that was, if anyone dared look up at him.

Moments later, the princess entered and also climbed the stairs onto the lofty roost. She wore a stunning jeweled gown embroidered with dragons and horses.

The emperor then summoned the evening's entertainment with a clap. A troupe of acrobats flooded into the arena and erected barricades to separate the evening's guests from the performance area. Ardeshir admired the flexibility and agility of these men and women as they performed death-defying flips.

Afterward the same performers carried in potted trees and bushes and set them upon the sand, as though to simulate a forest setting. The room's fiery lamps were extinguished and a row of clay lamps lit around the room's perimeter.

It was just as well that he didn't fill his plate, because that's when Liu arrived and encouraged Ardeshir to step forward. His young friend led him out of the room and took him into a small chamber where numerous weapons and costumes had been laid out.

"Choose how you will dress and how you will fight," Liu instructed.

"What do you mean?" Ardeshir asked.

"Tonight you will fight for the hand of the princess. To prove your honor before the emperor, you must conquer the beasts of his garden. You will be met by five foes of the emperor's choosing. You may choose six weapons, but each may only be used once." Liu gestured to the impressive array of battle gear. "If you live through these challenges, the princess is yours."

"What if I don't beat them all?"

Lui bowed. "If you die, then she will go to the general. Choose carefully because you will use the weapons against whatever enters the floor."

Ardeshir scrutinized the weapons on display. "I have need of one weapon which isn't here. The one you showed me after the leopard took your sister. You called it the fire medicine and crafted it by mixing together many powders. Is that available?"

"It has been waiting for a night like tonight," Liu said with a smile. "Use it very carefully. The princess wants *all* of you."

The unassuming young man picked up a woven bag from one of the tables and handed it to Ardeshir, who looked inside and nodded.

"I have one other weapon which you might find interesting," Liu said as he produced a metal throwing star. "That is, if we have a few minutes to train."

The terror that drove him over the next hour continued to beat after he was ushered back into the arena. Fear beat in his breast as he successfully dispatched lion, bear, and tiger with his javelin, sword, and crossbow. He heaved and gasped for air, grateful for all the training Yas had insisted on teaching him over the course of the past year, as the dead tiger was displayed by the acrobats. They carried the corpse around the circle for all the guests to see.

He calmed his breathing, loosened his limbs, and rotated his shoulders. He was given five minutes before the next foe, enough time to choose a weapon and tend to any injury he had sustained from the previous bout. The break also gave him the chance to bow low before the princess and find his courage.

What a bizarre way this was to win the woman he desired!

He almost didn't see his fourth opponent enter the arena. Perhaps it was the flicker of light out of the corner of his eye that alerted him. He pivoted, sensing rather than seeing the black cat, quick and confident as it prowled in the shadows, sure of its mode of attack and its victim's helplessness. It could not avoid snarling, the one act that so often paralyzed its prey.

Ardeshir laid his trap carefully. He hefted the woven bag Liu had given him and sprinkled the powder in a circle around him. The leopard watched warily as Ardeshir retrieved a clay lamp and chunk of roast donkey from one of the tables around the outside of the room.

He then stepped into the middle of the circle as the crowd grew restless. He knelt on one knee, cradling the lamp, and held it near the powder.

Before anything else could happen, chimes sounded from the emperor's dais and two acrobats with poles cartwheeled their way toward the leopard. It snarled and batted at the poles for a moment, but then it ignored them and decided to make its play for Ardeshir himself.

Ardeshir crouched low, holding only a dagger now. He deduced that this cat was used to chasing fearful, helpless prey. Perhaps it wouldn't know what to do with him. Ardeshir wouldn't follow any pattern it recognized.

The leopard now focused fully on him. It crept low to the ground, clinging to shadows as best it could.

Suddenly, it feigned a charge. Ardeshir stiffened as the beast lurched forward, then began circling him and the powder laid out around him. Ardeshir's heart raced, knowing that his life depended on a weapon he knew nothing about.

As the leopard stalked forward, its tail dead still, it entered the circle. Ardeshir then lowered the lamp and set the powder ablaze.

The leopard leaped as flames engulfed it on all sides. It stood mesmerized as Ardeshir backed toward the edge of the arena. The flames circled the cat closely until it was confined to the very center, huddled around the roasted meat. It looked down at the meal, now focused on the one sure source of food available to it.

Ardeshir stood along the wall watching the flame race. The spectators reacted in awe, surely having never witnessed such a display.

Eyeing the encroaching flames, the leopard sniffed at the meat and then batted it with its paw. It sank its jaws into the roast and pulled away, but not quick enough to avoid the explosion that suddenly rocked the arena.

The leopard disintegrated into pieces. Liu's fire medicine had done its work.

Instead of the roar of approval Ardeshir expected, there was dead silence in the assembly. He had unleashed a terror that would change the world.

No one uttered a sound as he walked to the tables and guzzled a mug of rice wine. His nerves were shot, his ears ringing from the blast. The terror he had witnessed from his own hand stunned him.

Regulating his breathing, he calmed himself with thoughts of the princess standing motionless in the boat on the pond.

And then he heard it: the sound of the bone flute filtering through the smoke, stillness, and terror. The acrobatic team raced around the arena, collecting parts of the leopard's carcass and repairing damage to the barricades. Not one of them came close to Ardeshir.

What enemy could be left for him to face? Perhaps the emperor would consider his efforts enough for one night.

When the period of rest was over, a figure stepped out of the darkness. It was the general.

Ardeshir waited to see whether Ban Chao would unleash the next animal. But instead the imposing man stood a dozen strides away, swinging his scimitar back and forth in a blur of motion.

"You killed my leopard," the general said. "Now I kill you."

Ardeshir grabbed one of the acrobat's discarded poles, tucked the dagger into his belt, and backed away. "I think you better talk to the emperor. I'm supposed to be fighting a fifth animal."

"I *am* the fifth animal. I know you come for my princess. No one can have her apart from me."

Reality dawned on Ardeshir that the General would be his final barrier to reaching the princess—and they would be fighting to the death.

He had already used his javelin, sword, and crossbow, and of course he couldn't reuse the fire medicine. Where was his sister when he needed her? No doubt she was preoccupied with the Persian chef somewhere. When he'd been invited by the princess to attend this banquet, and to stand up for her, he had imagined being granted an interview with the emperor or the council. Never had he imagined having to fight for his life!

The melody of the bone flute continued to filter through the smoke. The words of the princess filled his mind.

"I will be all you need."

But now he knew that he needed a higher power.

"The Way is the way," he said aloud. "The Way is the way."

The general extended his scimitar. "Whatever incantations you use are of no value. I have the power of the shamans and the leopard spirit filling me. I have consumed the root of invincibility so no death can come near." He threw a handful of bones on the ground at Ardeshir's feet. "The lives of your chief warriors have been taken in battle yesterday and added to me. You shall soon join them in their torment. The dark spirits fill me even now. What power can stand against me?"

Ardeshir stood with his pole planted firmly in the ground. "We have a story in our faith tradition," he said. "It is of a young man who faced a giant even taller than you. The giant defied the young man, his armies, and his God. It's never wise to trade the power of the God who controls heaven and earth for one who controls shadows and the minds of weak men."

"You come against me with a pole and a dagger." The general laughed. "You have foolishly used your weapons against lesser animals. I will slice you into the smallest pieces with my scimitar, find a new cub, and feed your flesh to it in front of the princess... who will be my wife."

Ardeshir reached into his robe and felt the three items hidden there: the metal throwing star Liu had given him, as well as a sling, and a rock. He'd used it to keep the horses in line during the journey, but it now seemed one of his only weapons against a soldier who seemed to grow taller the closer he got.

Could he really bet his life on a piece of leather and a rock? No. His real weapon was the God who guided that rock.

"You come against me with terror and with the sword of death, but I come against you in the name of the God who lives forever," Ardeshir declared. "You will be delivered into my hands. With your own sword, you will die in front of all these witnesses."

Ban Chao stepped closer and swung his sword—hard. Ardeshir sprang back and ran away.

"Coward!" yelled the general. "You not only dishonor the emperor, the princess, and all men… but you dishonor your own nation. Stand still and fight like a warrior."

The crowd erupted in sounds of displeasure. The pressure almost forced Ardeshir back into close proximity with the general.

Then the princess's words touched his spirit.

"Why are you trying to prove yourself to people who don't matter when you know it won't get you what you want?"

He backed away. In this kingdom so hungry for truth, truth would have to win him first.

Twice he felt the nick of the general's swirling blade as the man twirled and thrusted, calling down the vengeance of the gods. He ignored the small trickle of blood down his arm. He offered a prayer and felt in his pocket for the metal throwing star.

He dropped the pole, which clattered to the ground at his feet.

Instead he retrieved the throwing star, gripping it as Liu had taught him. Without hesitation he hurled it toward Ban Chao and caught him in the shoulder. He let out a great roar of pain as he yanked the star out of his own body and hurled it back. The razor-sharp weapon sliced sideways across Ardeshir's ribs as he dove out of the way. He staggered back to his feet, fear creeping through every limb.

He said another prayer of desperation.

Setting the rock in the pouch of the sling, Ardeshir swung it in the dim light. He doubted a single person would understand the motion of his hand, never mind the emperor or the princess from their elevated perch.

With yet another prayer, he unleashed the rock and heard its impact on flesh and bone.

"Awww!" The general clawed at his face and fell to his knees. "What demon have you sent on me?"

Ardeshir snatched up the pole at his feet and swung it hard across the general's neck. The man fell face down.

He used the general's own sword to finish the fight and separate his head from his body.

The acrobats tumbled into the arena to drag away the general's remains. All the lamps were lit as servants dumped buckets of sand over the pools of blood.

Ardeshir glanced up for a glimpse of the princess, but both she and the emperor had left behind empty chairs.

Blood dripped off his fingers and down his side as the room began to spin. He stumbled toward the tables and reached for a bowl of water. Darkness welcomed him.

Nineteen

The flickering candlelight and strong odor of horse left Ardeshir with no doubt about who was near. He would rather have smelled jasmine. His tongue felt thick and pain coursed through his side and right arm. He heard his own groaning, but it sounded otherworldly, muffled, distant.

"Shhh! Lie still, brother. You're still with us."

"Where am I?"

"Liu brought you here," Yas said. "You're in a hidden room at the back of his home. He sewed up your arm and side. You're feverish. Just rest."

"What happened?"

"You passed the test of five," Liu answered. "Now the council is waiting to see if you live. They are also debating whether it was a fair trial since you used unknown weapons against your opponents. If they consent to the outcome, you must present four noble truths to prove your character before the emperor."

"Where is the princess?"

"She awaits in seclusion until the final outcome." Liu lifted Ardeshir's head and raised a small bowl to his lips. "Here, drink this. It will ease the journey you must take toward healing."

That journey was unlike anything Ardeshir had ever taken before. Before his eyes, writhing dragons and serpents wrestled with fanged monkeys and winged horses. Amidst it all walked a serene figure of peace who often nodded and smiled in Ardeshir's direction. There was something alluring about this man in white who calmly faced the chaotic world around him. Ardeshir envisioned himself sitting at the feet of the one who would teach.

"I am truth," the one in white said. "I am the Way. Listen to me. Follow me."

In the morning, energy surged through Ardeshir's body and he stretched, yawning. Gone were those mythical creatures and strange terrors he had perceived in his dreams. The first fingers of dawn walked across the room until they rested on the figure sleeping beside him. It was Liu.

He touched his friend on the elbow. "Good morning!"

Liu stared up at the ceiling and sat up slowly. He nodded and smiled. "The shepherd of peace has healed you. You spoke much on your journey."

"The Way is the way," Ardeshir said. "He told me much about the Way. He *is* the Way."

"You have many truths to teach me," Liu said. "The council will see now that you live, and they will debate the outcome of the trial of five. You should begin to think of four noble truths worthy of a princess. I will get you something to eat so you are strong enough to face the council—and the emperor."

Liu bathed Ardeshir's wounds daily and applied a small paste over them. Healing scars formed protective sheaths over these badges of courage.

On occasion, Yas stopped by with offerings from the camp cook to supplement the food Liu's mother already provided.

A full week passed with little conversation from anyone until the day Ardeshir stepped out into the sunshine and sat on a stump in the garden near the koi pond.

"The guardians still aren't sure whether to permit me to enter the emperor's garden," Yas remarked as she arrived. "They hear rumors that you have magical powers and are afraid to displease you. Tell me, what did you do during your testing?"

Ardeshir raised his face to the sun and smiled. "I tried to do what you trained me to do," he said. "I faced my enemies, waited for them to attack, and exploited their weaknesses." He rubbed his scraggly goatee with his knuckles and chuckled. "I tried to make myself small to fan their confidence. I struck quickly when the opportunity came. I didn't hesitate to do what had to be done."

"What happened to my little brother?" Yas asked with a smile. "Lui said you used weapons unknown to the emperor's people and to the general."

"Surprise is a major advantage in any form. Come, walk with me. Liu says the emperor's spies must see that I'm strong and ready for what's next."

They soaked up the sunshine for several long minutes before Yas finally sought to satisfy her curiosity.

"I'm told you used an unknown weapon," she mused. "What possible weapon could you know that I don't?"

Ardeshir smiled. "Liu once showed me a fire medicine invented by his uncle. When fire is added to a small pile of powder, a mighty explosion is created. I spread that powder around the arena, then ignited it to destroy the leopard."

"I heard that explosion," Yas said. "In the camp, we wondered what might have happened. People in the market are still spinning tales of what a powerful wizard you have become."

Ardeshir held out his scarred arm. "You can see that I bleed like anyone. I had the right people teach me the right things at the right time. That's all."

"You almost sound wise," Yas said. "Perhaps what you just said should form the heart of the four noble truths you must present."

"Perhaps. I'm listening to a wise teacher who tells me what I need to know."

Yas looked around. "If you're talking about Liu, or even myself, I think you can do better."

"Don't worry. I wouldn't put that burden on you. If my life is on the line, I want to hear truth from someone who really *knows* it."

Another week passed with no word from the council on what their verdict might be, but there were subtle signs of change around the palace. The guardians no longer hesitated to allow Ardeshir and Yas to enter the gardens. Villagers stopped and nodded in deference to the brother and sister. Mysterious gifts appeared at their encampment. Ardeshir walked with his head held high, feeling increasingly confident that the council's judgment would fall in his favor.

Despite the change for Ardeshir and Yas, the traders, cataphracts, and outriders with the caravan continued to be treated as outsiders. A feeling of restlessness grew over the camp and the cataphract leader announced that they had decided to begin their trek home in two days, whether or not Yas or Ardeshir were ready to leave.

Yas negotiated for four days.

On the third day, a carriage accompanied by twenty guardians on horseback arrived at the camp from the palace. An ambassador alighted from the carriage, bowed to Ardeshir, and handed over a large roll of hemp paper with a wax seal.

"From the council," he declared.

Ardeshir had been working hard on his Mandarin but the extensive script still confounded him. He sent a messenger to bring the old man's daughter from the teahouse. In the meantime, the guardians waited patiently for his reply.

The young woman arrived dressed in her traditional blue with golden dragons emblazoned. She nodded in respect to him and accepted the scroll without explanation.

She bobbed her head as she scanned the message. "It say: 'Council agree that you live and general die. It say that council agree that you pass trial of five. Council disagree on whether you fight fair. Want explanation of fire medicine and how many weapons you use. If they agree, you share four noble truths."

The verdict seemed to represent a partial victory, but Ardeshir found that it produced even greater discouragement. What would it take to win the princess? He wasn't sure the effort was worth the trouble anymore. The rest of the caravan would be leaving in the morning, and it would be too dangerous to travel on his own. To remain might mean giving up his title and place in Persia.

Ardeshir turned back to the young woman. "Please explain the customs I need to understand before addressing the council."

"First, must have tea," she said.

A girl of about ten appeared from the carriage holding a set of small porcelain cups, intricately woven with blue dragons.

The girl nodded. "For the honorable one."

When the tea had been sampled, the old man's daughter set her cup aside and looked toward the palace.

"All things begin with sacrifice to ancestors, to country, and to spirits. Family is everything and you have come to take the most precious of family from our kingdom." She waited for his response. Not getting any. she took another sip of tea. "We believe we came from our ancestors and we will be ancestors for those who come after. We must honor those who came before. Sacrificing animals is important part of honor. On great river, we have festival of dragon boat and honor silkworm god." Another pause. Another sip. "Some honor mountain spirit and underground spirit. If we anger thunder God, we sacrifice pigs, chickens, geese, ducks, whatever we have." She stood and looked toward the patient guardians waiting nearby. "These men come from land of Dark Magpie. They think Dark Magpie will save us all. Almost time for sacrifice of bull at full moon." She turned toward him. "Pray to your God they not take you for their bull…"

The following day, Ardeshir rode outside the camp on horseback and waited for the palace guardians to assemble. Standing with the princess's hemp scroll in his hands, Ardeshir made his declaration.

"I will come now and make my declaration before the council," he said upon dismounting. "In the morning, I will leave this place whether I have spoken my four truths or not."

He swung up onto the back of his mount and followed the guardians toward the palace. On his last glance back, he noticed Yas standing in the middle of the pathway, hands open. She had no idea what he was doing.

When they neared the palace, the horsemen veered off the main road and followed a carefully groomed path toward a set of golden gates. A thick stream of golden chrysanthemums lined the way.

The gates swung open and Ardeshir followed the guardians toward the entrance of the Red Palace. He had never been to this part of the structure before, and as he reached the doors a young man dressed in scarlet robes took the reins of his horse—the same ambassador who had addressed them the previous day.

He swung down and followed the ambassador through a golden door.

He waited for an hour inside the palace, four strides from the gateway, composing himself for his grand entrance to the council. What could he say about the fire medicine? He didn't want to say anything that would endanger Liu? And how would he explain the sling? Did that count as a weapon, even though he had brought it himself?

The ambassador returned only to direct him to a chamber where he was instructed to change his clothing and bathe himself. The council would not be subjected to his shabby, smelly state. Four assistants scurried around, preparing a tub, scrubbing him down, rubbing ointment onto his skin, massaging him, and then dressing him in a brilliant golden robe with blue embroidered dragons.

Six guardians in full regalia arrived to escort him to his destination. On the way, they marched him around the paths of the koi pond, around the maze, and then down the cobblestoned pathway to the grand hall, the chamber where the council of truth reigned supreme.

The council consisted of twelve ancients with long grey beards and scarlet caps. Golden tassels dangled from the brim of their caps. They sat behind a long, raised table on elevated stools. Ardeshir's scroll lay open before them.

The council members' robes sparked a memory of the teashop. He had seen the old man returning there one day in such robes. The man had treated him with compassion. It was a shame he had decided to feed himself to the lions rather than remain for this moment. It would have been nice to have an ally.

A man stood on either end of the long table. The one on the right spoke first.

"I will speak for you, and my colleague will speak against you. So will we arrive at truth." He waited for a moment, as though composing himself. "You have come as a stranger into our midst, violating our customs and yet learning what is true and important. You have completed the trial of five with strange new weapons, yet you have survived. You have killed the general of the palace, yet you have attracted the heart of the princess." He took a few steps forward, crossing around to the front of the table. "You posed as a teacher of truth, yet we do not fully understand whether you have the truth we need to hear. You have brought chaos and violence into our sanctuary of peace, yet you have proved courageous and loyal. You have successfully brought us the horses desired by our emperor and restored honor to the Red Palace of the Han. I am placing my white stone in the basket to declare that I am satisfied that you should live and be given the chance to share your four noble truths."

With that, the man walked to the center of the table and dropped a white stone into the basket waiting there.

The other council member then raised a black stone for all to see.

"I stand for those opposed to the acceptance of this invader. With no regard for our traditions and sacred paths, he has violated custom after custom." He set the stone down and turned to the others seated at the grand table. He pointed at Ardeshir. "He handled the very princess herself and has not yet paid with his life. With no regard for the security of the emperor, he trespassed into the park of the wild on at least one occasion and came into our space with no good intent. Twice he has been disciplined by the guardians, yet still he has not learned respect for our ways. He brings evil magic into our peace and fought unfairly to destroy the very life of the general of the palace." He snatched up the black stone and raised it again. "With this stone, I say 'Enough!' to strangers destroying our way of life—and 'Enough!' to putting the noble lives of our leaders at risk. 'Enough!' to foreigners who tell us truth that violates our ears. 'Enough!' to renegades who bring inferior trade to steal the sacred values of silk and jade produced by our own sons and daughters."

He dropped his stone in the basket and returned to his place.

Everything within Ardeshir that fought for survival urged him to step forward and defend himself. But with a prayer to Yeshua, he bit his tongue and focused on the pain and metallic taste of blood seeping along his teeth.

The basket was passed along the table, with each member dropping in either a black or white stone. No other council member offered any explanation as to why certain stones were deposited.

When the basket was finished travelling the length of the table, the palace's head guardian stepped up to Ardeshir and stripped him of his robe. Ardeshir's hands were tied behind his back and he was led to a single block in the center of the room.

"Kneel and place your neck on the block," the guardian commanded. "If the black stones are most, I will make this quick. If the white stones are most, you will receive your robes back and share your truths with the emperor."

Again, everything within Ardeshir screamed for a chance to defend himself. He focused instead on attempting to pray. Images of all his transgressions tumbled through his mind and he fought to speak words of reasonable explanation.

Still he knelt quietly, swallowing his words, staring at the sandy floor in front of him. Incense, perhaps frankincense, wafted gently across his nostrils, soothing him.

The sound of the gong startled him and he realized how badly his hands were shaking behind his back. His jaw was tight and his teeth clenched together. His whole body felt gripped in an icy shroud.

"Hear the verdict of the council of truth," a voice called out. "White stones, six. Black stones, six."

A tie! What did that mean?

The voice continued. "The emperor, the grand discerner of all truth, the wise and noble discerner of true reality, the hope of our people, the invincible patron of immortality, he will now cast his deciding stone for or against the life of this foreigner."

It took an hour. The cramps in Ardeshir's back, thighs, and shoulders begged him to call down the mercy of the guardian with the sword poised above him to end it quickly. For the lengthy wait could only mean one thing: the father had ignored the heart of his daughter and the end was now at hand.

Why had he been so stupid as to return? Farzana would have been a loyal wife and fine mother to his children. Mariam, from Caesarea, may have been persuaded to understand who he truly was—not a beggar, but a prince. Life with Yas would have been awkward, but at least they'd be alive, supporting each other.

He fought for the calming presence of the peaceful teacher in white who had walked serenely in the midst of his dream chaos. Yeshua's face finally appeared to him with a joyful smile as though to say, "Not yet, my friend!"

A few moments later, the voice sounded again. "The hand of the conveyer of all truth has rendered the final verdict for us all to accept. We have a white stone. The prisoner will live and share his four noble truths."

The lead guardian grabbed Ardeshir by the hair and pulled his head up.

"Stand up," the man intoned. "You will live."

Ardeshir's wrists were freed from the ropes and he was guided by two lesser guardians back to the preparation room. His legs wobbled like rubber, his breaths escaped in short, convulsive sobs, and tears raced down his cheeks.

"Be grateful, warrior, to the emperor who has spared you," the guardian added before leaving him in peace. "Speak noble truths worthy of his ears."

A masseuse soon appeared to manhandle his legs, back, shoulders, and arms to restore circulation. He was then released to the chamberlains, who dressed him again in his yellow robe. His mind was too scrambled to fathom how he could present four noble truths worthy of the emperor, the discerner of all truth, but the time had come at last.

Twenty

Having already knelt before the golden throne inlaid with ivory and emeralds on a previous occasion, and having survived, Ardeshir regulated his breathing and controlled his thoughts. Fresh chrysanthemums surrounded the dais. The earthy herbal aroma still hovered in the air.

He continued with his face down and palms flat against the tiles while the emperor took his seat. Ardeshir sniffed hard for the scent of jasmine but failed to find his inspiration.

"Your people have left you," a strong voice declared. "You are alone and at our mercy. Are you wise enough to stay, or does your foolishness prove they were wise to leave you behind?"

Whose voice was this? The emperor's, or a member of his council? Ardeshir turned his palms up to indicate his desire to speak.

"Speak!" the voice commanded.

"I will be where I am at all times," he said. "I live at the mercy of the hand who holds mercy." He turned his palms back to the floor.

"Well said," the voice replied. "Speak your four noble truths and prove you are worthy of mercy. Speak them one at a time so we may record them and ponder their worth."

Ardeshir turned his palms up.

"Speak your first truth."

"Truth lives embodied in one but is discerned by the learned alone," he began.

Minutes passed. Sweat began to gather under Ardeshir's palms against the tiles. He longed to wipe them dry.

"The first is now recorded," the voice confirmed. "Speak the second truth."

The words tangled in his mind as he rearranged, edited, added to, and then settled on what he had to say.

"Breath and life are given by one but enjoyed by all."

"The second is now recorded," the voice said. "Speak the third truth."

"Truth sees all, knows all, discerns all, leaving nothing to chance or folly."

Once the words were spoken and recorded, it was too late to change them.

Truth speaker, speak to me, he prayed.

"The third is now recorded. Speak your final truth."

"The Way is the way and no one knows it apart from those to whom it is told."

Moments passed.

"The fourth is now recorded." A short hesitation. "We shall discuss the weight and wisdom of these truths to see if they are worthy of consideration. They are a small price to pay toward the worth of my daughter."

It was him!

He had now gotten his wish for an audience with the emperor, and it had been nothing like he'd dreamed. There had been no mediator to sift his words or direct his thoughts.

What would it mean to wed a princess of the Han? Could he serve as a link between the Persian and the Han kingdoms?

The shadows of evening passed and a cool breeze travelled along the floor. Still he did not move.

After a great deal of time had passed, he peeked up along the floor and saw no sandaled feet. However, the unmistakable melody of the flute floated into the room from the gardens outside.

Would he ever get the chance to return the heart he had taken? Would the princess ever be satisfied, or even happy, with a Persian prince? Would she leave the Red Palace of the Han emperor to travel to a land with a foreign tongue and foreign people?

First, he had to await the approval of his four noble truths.

Lui found him the next morning meditating by the koi pond. The three carvers sat nearby shaping their own creations.

"Truth speaker!" Lui began.

Ardeshir opened one eye.

Lui crouched down beside him and whispered, "The emperor has ordered your sister and the trade caravan to return to Persia. If you leave, you will have lost your chance with the princess."

Ardeshir rose to his knees. "What? Yas wouldn't leave me. How did you hear this?"

"The Persian chef told me."

Ardeshir sprang to his feet. "I've got to talk with Yas. This can't be good. She needs to wait a little longer."

"Rest your mind, your body, and your heart," Lui said. "Truth will prevail. Go back and wait."

Instead of heeding his friend's advice, Ardeshir ran toward the Persian camp outside the village. Four guardians stood at the exit, fully armed with swords and javelins.

He looked past them toward the camp. The sounds of the Persians were gone. How had they moved so quickly without him?

There had to be another way out of this garden.

Returning to the camp felt empty. Even Yas had gone and he had no one with whom to share his experiences. He wandered back over the koi bridge and stopped outside Lui's home. Quiet laughter rose from within, but he turned to walk away.

"Prince, friend," Liu called. "Return. This is your home. We have another cup for you."

The evening of friendship washed away many of the dark weights that tore at his mind and soul.

"I had nowhere else to go," he confessed as the night wore on. "I need a family."

"Leopard killer is hero," said Liu's father. "Now, no live in fear. Night is peace. No snarls." He nodded his head the tiniest bit. "Prince Shir welcome here."

"Thank you, Zhao Chu," Ardeshir said. "Your son has become a hero. You can be very proud of him. He has become like a brother to me."

Their dinner was simple but filling, and afterward Ardeshir and Liu walked around the pond. Darkness settled over the garden and the stars shone with brilliance.

Liu pointed up. "When I was a boy, my father used to tell me that all the stars were the eyes of leopards looking down to eat me. I could never go outside. The general has kept us in fear as long as I can remember."

Ardeshir reclined on the ground and stared upward, imagining the constellations and their epics playing out far above in the heavens.

"We used to hear stories of how the Magi's militia would scoop us up and feed us to the lions if we stepped off our farm at night," Ardeshir said. "No matter where children grow up, I imagine their parents find stories to keep them from straying." He sat up and looked across the koi pond toward the palace. "I wonder if she will come with me when I leave this place. I should talk with the Persian chef to see if he has had any more conversations with her."

"You cannot talk with the Persian chef," Liu said.

"Why not? I have earned the right to talk to anyone in this garden. I could talk to him right now, couldn't I?"

He got up and started walking toward the small bridge that led to the palace kitchen.

"You walk that way for nothing," Liu called after him.

Ardeshir kept walking, though. Who was this former gardener to tell him what he could or couldn't do? He was a prince. He had killed the leopard and the general. He had succeeded in the trial of five. The villagers now clearly respected him. If all went well, he would soon marry the princess.

At the kitchen door, he rapped with his knuckles and waited. And when no one came, he knocked louder. What Mandarin greeting was there to get people's attention at night?

As he backed off from the door, searching for other entrances, a dainty figure stepped out from an alcove.

"Hello," the woman said. "How I help?"

"I need the Persian chef," Ardeshir said firmly. He realized that he hadn't even learned the man's name. "The one who cooks for the emperor. Call him so I can talk with him."

"Man gone."

"Gone where?" Ardeshir probed.

"Gone home."

"Where does he live?"

"Persia."

"Persia?"

"Yes."

"Where is he here?"

"Not here."

"Where does he stay?"

Liu cleared his throat behind Ardeshir and Ardeshir pivoted to face his friend.

"What is wrong with her?" Ardeshir asked. "I'm trying to find out where the Persian chef is staying and she won't tell me. I got rid of the general! There's no more reason to be afraid."

"She's not afraid," Liu said. "She is trying to tell you that the Persian chef left for Persia with your sister. You were so busy that you missed the relationship they were building. They aren't far, though, if you borrow a horse and chase them."

Ardeshir stood with his mouth agape. "My sister with the chef? How did I miss that? How can I go now when the council is so close to deciding whether I can marry the princess?"

Liu traipsed back across the bridge. "You may have a longer wait than you think. If the truths you gave are deep, the council can talk, debate, think, and decide over many days or weeks. The longer they talk, the better for you."

"But I can't wait," Ardeshir said. "I need to marry the princess and catch up with my sister before the caravan reaches Hindustan. It would be too dangerous for me and the princess to travel on our own."

"Prince, friend, you are not very observant. The princess's wedding lasts for one year, to test if her husband is good enough. If you want to marry, you should find a place to stay, learn Mandarin well, and understand how the emperor thinks about truth."

His heart slammed in his chest and he gasped for breath, pressing hard over his heart. This was like being thrown into the animal park with no escape.

What did it matter anymore about what the emperor thought was truth? What good would it do for him to fight a losing battle?

"There is much to do to prepare for your wedding to a princess," Lui said. "You must learn to speak her heart language."

"Can you teach me?" Ardeshir asked.

"I teach you first about the lord and lady of the house," Liu said. "You live with the emperor. The oldest man is the lord of the house and takes care of the property, matters of war, and everything outside the walls. The lady is the oldest woman and decides everything inside the walls, such as the food, servants, furniture, comfort, and celebrations." He waited for Ardeshir to fall into step next to him. They walked alongside each other. "In the first year, the emperor will be the oldest man in your house. You will do as he says. The emperor's wife will be the oldest lady. The princess will do what she says. Before you run your own kingdom, it is best to learn how to run a kingdom from the one who knows all truth… and who can teach you all truth."

Ardeshir dragged his sandals through the grass. "I'm not sure I can last through all that," he said. "Do you have a horse I can borrow?"

"Sleep one more night. Decisions made in a hurry only lead to greater worry."

"Okay. One more night."

A week later, Ardeshir was continuing to "give it one more night"—every night. However, on the day he firmly intended to leave, he readied his horse outside the palace gates.

Before he could depart, the melody of the bone flute drifted across the hedges and tickled his ears. He walked trancelike back to the pond and stood on the bridge watching the window where the princess played.

A brief movement was all it took for him to stare the afternoon away.

The following day, and the day after, he repeated the same pattern.

"What are you waiting for?" Liu asked on the third day.

"I just need a chance to talk and explain myself. I can't sit and wait forever."

"Not forever." Liu chuckled. "How long does the farmer wait for the apple after planting its seed? Love is like that. Take time to harvest the fruit."

"Can you get her a note?" Ardeshir asked.

"She knows you are here. She will let you know what she is thinking when you need to know it."

Ardeshir slammed his fist onto the bridge railing. "I am not a mouse to be played with."

"What does that mean?"

"I fought for her. I won the trial of five. I gave the emperor my four noble truths."

"And you still live."

Ardeshir shook his head in frustration. "Is this what you had to go through for your own wife?"

"I didn't want to marry the princess."

The palace gong sounded the next morning as the sun rose. *Gong—gong—gong.* Moments later, Liu stood over Ardeshir's reed mat, smiling.

"Come, prince, friend. The council has decided on your four noble truths."

Ardeshir rolled out of bed. "I thought you told me that the longer they took, the better." He donned his robe and slipped on his sandals. "Does this mean they might say no?"

"We don't know," Liu admitted. "Maybe you need to go home and come back next year."

"Can they do that?"

"The council is the council. They can do what they want, but mostly they do what the emperor wants."

"So if the emperor doesn't want to lose his daughter to a foreigner, there is no hope." Ardeshir sighed dramatically. "I should have gone with my sister. What a fool I am, trying to impress someone who can't be impressed."

"Is that what you were doing?" Liu asked. "Trying to impress someone who can't be impressed?"

"Why are you asking me this? He's your emperor. I'm a prince with my own kingdom to run. I need to get back and do what I'm supposed to do."

He hurried outside into the morning air. Numerous people were already crossing the bridges and heading for the emperor's palace.

"Where are you keeping my horse?" Ardeshir asked.

Liu stepped in front of him and bowed. "Too late for a horse. The guardians come for you."

There was no question about it: twelve guardians in bright red garb were marching across the bridge over the koi pond, moving toward him like a river of blood.

Paralysis set into Ardeshir's limbs. Everything inside screamed for him to run, but he remained still as the troop formed around him. He then fell into step, unable to stop himself from following them toward the palace.

The march flowed through the golden gates and into the same arena where the trial of five had been fought and won. Bright lamps lit the hall and open windows drew in the streaming sunlight. An ornate cedar table in the middle of the room boasted the carved images of dragons, snakes, monkeys, oxen, pigs, and other members of the animal kingdom.

The council of twelve, now dressed in white, sat rigidly in place at the front of the hall. The basket of judgment, where the black and white stones were placed, sat in the center.

One of the ancients, sitting near the basket, rose and beckoned Ardeshir to stand before them. Behind him, the guardians all withdrew, leaving him to face his fate alone.

The prayers he had formulated over days were reduced to one word: *"Help."*

"Welcome, prince of Persia," the ancient spoke in near flawless Persian. "By the mercy of the emperor, you were spared after the trial of five. By the mercy of the emperor, your gift of horses was accepted as adequate for trade. By the mercy of the emperor, you have been permitted to stay in the gardens within the range of hearing his daughter's flute." He pulled the basket of judgment toward himself. "But not even the emperor can show mercy if your four noble truths do not pass the test of wisdom." He gazed with piercing fire at Ardeshir. "You have brought us babblings like a child and expected us to swallow them whole. We sought an ocean and you brought us a puddle in which to wade. Is there nothing of depth among your people?"

The shaking in Ardeshir's knees increased as he clamped his teeth to keep the shaking from spreading to the rest of his body. To have come so far and still have failed? It was too much to bear. Where was the Almighty when it mattered?

He raised his eyes to the throne of the emperor and saw in the seat beside him the sparkle of a beautiful gown dazzling with dozens of prisms.

The princess had come to watch his final moments.

Twenty-One

The ancient one pulled on his chest-length snowy beard. "We wonder whether you think we are simple-minded children. Or perhaps you think that noble truth means thought with no meaning. Perhaps the wisdom of Persia has been lost. We say that maybe the prince is tired from the trial of five. Maybe distracted by thought of the princess. And maybe he's sad to see his sister go alone."

The man glanced briefly toward the exalted throne.

"We will try to find a reason for the white stone as it concerns truth number one," he continued, picking up a roll of hemp paper and pondering its contents. "You say, 'Truth lives embodied in one but is discerned by the learned alone.' If we say this is not noble truth, it may seem like we are not learned. Truth lives in the emperor, but maybe you mean someone else. If only one embodies truth and the emperor is not the one, then you cannot live." He pulled on his beard with one hand, and then the other. "We ask each other why the prince would risk life and love in the trial of five but throw his life away with simple words which have no truth. Maybe there is a deeper truth. So we wait and take more time to hear your teaching. We grant no stone yet for this one."

The ancient one ran his finger over the scroll again.

"For the second truth, you say, 'Breath and life are given by one but enjoyed by all.' Again, this simple thought fights against the truths we already know. The gods and spirits we know are more than one. What more are you saying? No stone yet for this."

He finally reached for the basket of stones and held up a white stone.

"We grant a white stone for number three truth: 'Truth sees all, knows all, discerns all, leaving nothing to chance or folly.' We think this is simple, but it is true when it is true."

He pulled the roll closer and unfurled it a little.

"'The Way is the way and no one knows it apart from those to whom it is told.' We want to give a black stone for this one, but each time we reach for the black stone we find instead that it is white. This is a deep magic. We cannot refuse, but we need to hear more from you on this matter."

What does all this mean? Ardeshir asked himself as the hall fell silent. Two stones with no decision, one white out of sympathy, and one possibly white if only he could explain the magic of it more clearly. *Am I now a prisoner without options?*

He bowed to the floor and opened his palms.

"Speak, Prince Shir," the ancient one intoned. "What will you say of the council's decision?"

"How does the council choose to untangle this knot of indecision?" Ardeshir finally spoke. "And what is the hope for the princess?"

"I will answer that," another voice boomed. Ardeshir looked up in shock to realize that the emperor had spoken. "When the council cannot decide, it is up to the emperor to declare what is true. I have decided. If your truths are not clear falsehoods to the wisest of men, they are worthy of further consideration. You shall teach the council and the princess what they must understand. When you are finished, we will talk at the chrysanthemum throne."

The cool stones on Ardeshir's forehead, nose, and chin distracted him from the heat racing through the rest of his body. How long would this process take? What if the council and princess refused to listen and understand the truths he embraced?

He finally understood why the rest of the caravan had left without him.

Later that afternoon, Ardeshir found himself escorted out of the palace and deposited at the golden gates. He shook his head as he looked up over the roof of the Red Palace.

"Yeshua, what are you doing with me now?" he moaned.

He didn't have long to wait for the answer. A guardian quickly arrived to escort him to the teaching plaza where he had first taught the princess more than a year ago.

The chrysanthemum throne sat where it always had, surrounded by a sea of flowers. Was there another decision to be made in this place, another lesson to be taught and learned?

He knelt and waited. It had been so long since the first time he waited in this space like this.

"You are now a teacher again," the guardian told him. "You must teach the truths the council needs to understand."

Left alone here, Ardeshir knelt in his teaching position and waited. Instead of the council, however, he heard the softest whisk of presence waft across his spirit. The scent of jasmine tickled his nostrils.

It was enough to make him sob.

"You live," the princess said from behind him.

"I live," he replied without turning. "Your flute gave life to my soul, hope to my mind, strength to my body."

"It is why I play." She came closer and loomed over him. She laid her hand on his head. "Thank you for returning my heart. It has found peace."

He raised his gaze. "I am happy to give it back to you."

"My heart is not like it was." She moved away and sat on the throne. "You changed it. It has known fear in the trial of five. It has known confusion in considering your truths. It has known anger, because you observe me like a man but keep me at a distance."

"Oh one on whom the full moon shines... one who captures the beauty of gardens and flowers... one who brings the joy and life of the freest of birds... I am honored to teach the soul of the Han Empire."

A coy smirk caught the corners of her mouth. "I see you learned something from the general before you killed him. I liked when he said such things to keep control. You gave me my heart back so you can keep your own control. You can call me Lu Hou."

Ardeshir nodded. "But isn't this name the seed of your soul? Isn't it much too intimate for a teacher to speak with his student?"

She slipped back off the throne and moved toward him. "Perhaps this teacher is also a man who must know the one to whom he speaks." She extended her hand and waited for him to rise. "I didn't know you were so tall."

The princess stepped aside and motioned for him to follow.

"What must I teach you?" he asked, falling into step as they approached a path that would take them through the garden.

"What else do teachers do but speak of truth?" Stooping to pick up a pebble, she tossed it into the koi pond and watched the ripples. "Truth will spread where it will and reach the shores of unexpecting minds."

"I can speak about the truth of love, peace, joy, hope, family, and life beyond this kingdom."

"I will learn these things well," she said. "My lessons begin tomorrow. But now it is time for me to play my flute for you. I must hurry to my room. Listen well to the song of my heart."

There was a definite difference in the way Lu Hou took to his teachings now versus a year ago. Perhaps it was because she now insisted he teach in Persian, which forced her to concentrate more. Although when she needed clarity, she switched to Mandarin.

Day after day, the two of them sat in the plaza with the chrysanthemum throne as numerous workers, guardians, and bypassers stopped to listen. For Ardeshir, it was as if the world faded away as the two of them drew together their minds and souls. There was little sense of superiority or arrogance in the princess. She felt free to ask questions and debate his points.

"Why are you so eager to learn from me now?" he asked. "Before, you seemed determined to question everything I said."

She sat lotus-like, focused. "You notice my learning. It is good, yes?"

"Yes! But why the change?"

"You have changed too, but I know not why. You disappeared as a foolish teacher and returned as a brave warrior and humble sage. You also brought back my heart."

"What about the change in you?"

"No change in me. I'm still the emperor's daughter. I still play the flute. Only now I have my heart."

"But you listen to me."

"Yes. I listen hard," she said. "The council says that if I explain your four noble truths well, I can take you as my husband. We can then join our two kingdoms—everyone happy, wealthy, and wise."

"What do you mean when you say that we'll join the kingdoms?"

She unwound her legs from the lotus position and rose to stretch as she looked toward the palace. "I am a student without answers. I know that these four noble truths must be taught and known before marriage can happen. You teach, I listen."

He followed as she got up to pluck a golden flower and place it in the nest of hair coiled on the side of her head.

"I thought that you were trying to understand the truth so you could believe," he said.

"Believe what?"

"Believe the truth."

She plucked a second flower and handed it to him. "First we know truth. The flower is beautiful. Next we understand truth. What is beauty?" She smiled coyly. "Then we believe what is beautiful."

He nodded. She was teaching him, but was she also toying with him? If she had to know these truths well enough to teach and convince the council that she understood them, it meant he needed to change his strategy. She had shown him the way she learned: know truth, understand truth, believe what is true.

But perhaps he needed to change the order.

Holding the flower, he focused on it. "Define beauty, accept beauty, embrace beauty," he said.

He was so focused on this revelation that he walked off into the garden, leaving her open-mouthed behind him.

The process now made sense. The council questioned his ability to communicate truth not so they could accept what he had to say but to test his ability to teach the woman to whom he wanted to express his love. If he could get out of his own mind and find a way to awaken the mind of another, he would prove himself to those who charted his future.

"Yeshua, I need you to teach me *how* the Way is the way. I need you to define it so others can accept it and embrace it."

"Prince Shir! Prince Shir!"

Ardeshir whirled to find the princess standing on the path behind him, her hands opened toward him.

"Why did you leave me?" she called. "Did I offend you? Am I not learning? Will you steal my heart again?"

He held up the flower. "No, Lu Hou. You did not offend me. I was thinking about your wisdom and how to better speak truth to you so you can convey it to the council." He stepped toward her. "And this is the first time I have heard you call me by my name."

"You are pleased that I use your name?" She lowered her hands and her eyes. "But you are a teacher. I must show respect."

He came to a stop right in front of her and for the first time dared to reach out and touch her chin. "Look at me, Lu Hou. When you use my name in my kingdom, you are showing me all the respect I need."

She gazed so deeply into his eyes that it shook him, as if she had seen to the depths of his soul. He blinked and she stepped away.

"One day, we will see each other," she said. "If you teach me well, we won't have to wait too long." She backed away. "One more problem. You need to learn Mandarin to teach me. Then I will know for sure what you say is true in my heart."

"Will you teach me?"

"Liu will teach you. I learned Persian and hear truth. Now you must learn Mandarin and teach truth."

She continued to walk away.

"Will you still come to be with me?" he called after her.

She turned on the path. "I will return when you are ready to teach my heart. I will play my flute so you don't forget to learn quick."

Moments later, she reached the palace and the door closed behind her.

Liu stepped onto the pathway in front of him. "Mandarin is a language for the soul," he said. "You will learn quickly so the princess stays happy. I will teach it to you fast so the emperor is happy too."

Ardeshir focused hard and spoke all the Mandarin he knew. "Hello. I am called Ardeshir. Very beautiful."

Liu nodded. "It is a start. Now, be a child and we will learn how to walk with our tongue in the morning. A guardian will teach you how to be a warrior in the afternoon."

"First teach me about your healing," Ardeshir said.

Liu motioned him toward a shed near his home. It was the same one whose roof Ardeshir had climbed onto in an effort to avoid the leopard.

"In here," Liu said. "I will show you healing."

Once through the door, Ardeshir was stunned to see a butchered dog hanging from the ceiling next to a hawk.

Liu pointed toward the dog's carcass. "We say that of all the birds in the sky, quail is the most delicious. And among beasts, dog is the most delicious. The dog's liver is sweet, bitter, salty, and mild. It fixes one's insides. The heart is sweet, sour, salty, and mild. It improves blood flow." He then moved on to touch the hawk. "The meat of the hawk takes away evil. Ashes protect from ghosts. Dung and liquor release bad energy. Tiger bones are good for the joints. Owl hair and insides, when fried in oil, can cure mosquito fever."

In a dish lay a disemboweled toad.

Liu pulled the dish closer. "Toads are good for relieving fever and poison. Even ulcers. Snake meat is like magic for the organs and keeps the blood moving. It also cures the cough and makes one's eyes bright."

Ardeshir backed away. "I think I've heard enough. Just don't use that stuff on me."

Liu smiled. "Too late, Prince Shir. I've already used it."

Twenty-Two

The next three months crawled and sprinted by at the same time. Immersing himself in intense language learning and equally intense battle skills kept Ardeshir's mind and body sharp. Each day at noon, as he transitioned from tongue-twisting to the fighting arts, the bone flute played its increasingly chipper melodies. And each evening, as he rested by the pond, the tunes eased his spirit.

But his heart grew restless as his Mandarin improved. He soon began to sense that it was good enough to begin teaching the princess about the four noble truths.

Lu Hou must have known the time was right before he did. As the bee-eaters flitted from tree to tree and the garden filled with song in the first rays of dawn, she sat in her lotus position. Ardeshir looked around for Liu, but his language teacher was nowhere in sight. He stood in the teaching space beside the koi pond, drinking in her form like a healed blind man glimpsing a glorious sunset for the first time.

She made no effort to stop him. The sun rays kissed the petals of the chrysanthemum in her hair and the sheen of her ebony locks glistened. The blue robe surrounded her with an aura unlike anything he had seen before. He hardly dared to believe his moment had come.

He attempted to approach her from behind but stopped five steps away.

"You can feel it like I can," she breathed.

Why should he be surprised? There was something otherworldly about her ability to sense the nuances of space, time, nature, and relationship.

"Are you ready to learn?" he asked.

"I am ready to be married to you," she responded with a smile. "Teach me as quickly as you can. Don't waste your words. One way or another, I shall convince the council that the time is right."

He sat on the mat which she had placed in front of her. She gazed deeply into his eyes and he let her look. He had cleansed away the debris of anger, grief, bitterness, and resentment. If there was anything else for her to see, he was ready to deal with it.

As if in response, she dipped her chin and breathed deeply.

"Your scent has changed," she said. "There is no more horse, milk, or ash in your sweat." She breathed in again. "Rose petals crushed in water, honey, lemon... and a touch of lye."

"It seems everyone except me knew about this. The maids laid out a special bath and robe for me. I thought I might have to talk with the council next."

"Only me. Please begin, and don't stop until I understand everything."

The serenity on her face, fullness of her lips, and stillness of her posture served to distract him even more from his task.

"How can I teach beauty to beauty itself?" he asked. "How can I teach peace to the one at peace?"

"The Way is the way! Start there and go backwards through the four noble truths. Others have spoken of truths which involve suffering and desire, but my heart is not aligned with them. You bring a different understanding of truth, which I must know." She opened her eyes and smiled. "Not just so I can marry you, but so we can be one in the rhythm of our ways. And so the council will give the emperor permission for me to leave if necessary. What must I know first?"

He gently touched her chin with his knuckle and settled himself. "First, we must define the Way. The Way is a person. His name is Yeshua. He is the Way, the Truth, the Life. There is no way but him."

The panic in her eyes, the increased rate of her breathing, and the tension in her arms betrayed her effort to absorb this truth.

She closed her eyes, regulated her breathing, focused on her pose, and then let out a long sigh.

"Definition is the first step in the journey," she said. "To define is to set the path you will walk. We do not ask to believe yet—only to know and understand."

Ardeshir plucked the flower from Lu Hou's hair and waved it under her nose. "Is this flower a chrysanthemum because of its fragrance, its shape, its color, its beauty, or because we have taken all those realities and defined them as chrysanthemum?"

She nodded. "To define is to take all that *is* of one thing and proclaim it as true." She opened one eye and smiled. "Am I a good student or are you a good teacher?"

He returned the flower to her hair. "We will see the answer when we are married. Now we will focus on the beginning. All that you see has been created by a personal Creator."

"All that I see is from a Creator," she repeated. "Even the general and his leopard?"

"Yes!"

"What about love?"

"Yes!"

Lu Hou set her jaw and laid her open hands on her knees. "I receive what you say. We walk this path together. The Way is a person. The Creator is a person."

By the late afternoon, Lu Hou had wrestled with her place in a visible and invisible world. She had wrestled with humanity's alienation from their Creator. She had listened to story after story of human history.

Afterward two guardians arrived to escort her back to the teaching plaza with the chrysanthemum throne near the koi pond. It was a covered open space in which the couple could bid farewell to each other.

For two weeks, they sat undisturbed each day wrestling with a worldview the princess had never before conceived.

"This idea will never be understood by my people," she said. "Is this the invention of Romans?"

Ardeshir reached for the pile of hemp paper he had been collecting each day. With a quill, he drew out several Mandarin characters.

"The truth of the stories I tell are already hidden in your own language," he said. "Look at the parts of each pictograph. You read the word and tell me its parts."

"It says *migrate*, and there are four parts. Great. Division. West. Walk."

"Many years ago, all peoples lived in one place, close to my home. They wanted to make themselves great. The Creator was unhappy and divided them by assigning them different languages. Your people came from the west, from my home, on a long walk. This is the true story."

"So we are one family separated by time and place."

"Yes! Do you see the word *west*?" he asked. "What parts make up that word?"

She traced the script with her pointer finger. "Three parts. One. Person. Closed garden."

"Like the emperor's garden. It is the idea of the first man created in this world. He was placed in a closed garden like this one."

Lu Hou laid out the next word. "It says *create*. Two parts. To talk and to walk."

"What parts do you see in the character for *to talk*?" Ardeshir asked.

She moved the manuscript closer to her. "Three parts. Dust. Breath. Alive."

"This tells us how the Creator made us," he said. "He shaped us from dust, breathed into us, and made us alive."

"This is a strange teaching. What else did you write?" She snatched up the pile of papers and began to work through them. "Word for God. Three parts. Reveal. Man. Closed garden."

She looked up expectantly.

"God the Creator revealed himself to the man in the closed garden," he told her.

"Next one is *blessing*. Four parts. God. One. Man. Closed garden."

"It was a blessing for God to be with the one man in the closed garden," Ardeshir said.

Lu Hou stared into his eyes and then looked back at the next character. "Desire... want... necessity. Two parts. West. Woman."

"We see that the God who blessed the one man in the closed garden met his need by adding a woman for him."

The princess was now beaming. "It is our story. The Creator made a beautiful garden for the emperor. He brought man of the dust with a blessing from the west. He gave him a woman. Me."

Ardeshir leaned back and smiled. "The first story I'm telling you about wasn't our story, but it sure does sound like it when you put it like that. This story is written in your characters many, many years ago. You bring out the truth in your own language."

Her frown took him by surprise. She was staring hard at the next paper.

"The next word says *forbidden*. Two parts. Two trees. Command." She laid the paper aside. "Not a good word for us."

He itched his chin with his knuckles. "It is a hard word. It means that the Creator provided a choice for the man and woman through a command. They could not eat from one of the trees."

"That's okay. We won't eat from the wrong tree. Which one is it?" She stood up and looked around the garden.

He stood with her. "It was a tree in the middle of the closed garden, not this one. Read the next word."

"Dark one. Evil one. I don't know this word." She lifted the paper closer to her face. "Four parts. Life. Secret. Closed garden. Man."

"It speaks of a secret one who lives and who came into the closed garden with the man. He is a bad one. We call him the devil."

She threw the paper toward the scrap holding the word *forbidden*. The page fluttered in the wind toward the edge of the teaching plaza.

"The bad one does not go far enough." She walked over and kicked the paper onto the grass.

Ardeshir bent over and picked up the next paper in the pile she had left behind. "Here's another you won't like. It says *tempter*. It has three parts that come together. Can you see them?"

Lu Hou walked closer. "Cover. Two trees. Dark one, the devil." She looked out toward the koi pond. "Let me guess. The dark one uses two trees to hide in."

She carefully walked back to where the abandoned paper had fallen, the one with the word *forbidden* written on it, and placed it together with the page reading *tempter*.

"The dark one is like the general and his leopard eating the poor." She glanced at the next word. "Desire. Made of two parts. Two trees. Woman." She moved the word to the bottom of her pile of pages. "The woman wants something in the two trees."

"Yes!" he said.

"The next one does not make sense," she said. "Pain. Made of two parts. Piece. Two trees."

"The man and woman took a piece from one of the two trees and were given pain," he explained. "There is one more word for today."

"Me. Two parts. Hand. Spear."

"Remember that the Creator made the first man in the closed garden from dust and then gave him a woman to meet his desire. This Creator gave a command and choice to the man and the woman, but the dark one secretly came into the closed garden and deceived them. They had to leave the garden and were given pain. Because of this, the pain comes on me, on all of us."

Lu Hou nodded. "It is a good place to stop. I know now that we can never leave the emperor's garden, or else we will be in pain. You have destroyed the dark one, so we are safe. We will have many babies here."

She got up and walked away with a smile on her face.

After she had gone, Ardeshir slumped on his mat and lowered his head into his hands. Teaching the truth, that the Way was the way, was turning out to be far more complicated than he had imagined.

It took three days to straighten out the tangled mess created by the misunderstanding on that first day of teaching. By then, both of them were anxious about the delay in their relationship.

"Teach me about more words," Lu Hou said as they returned to their lesson.

"We need to talk about the Way," Ardeshir handed her a new piece of hemp paper. "Here is one more word."

"Rightness," she said. "Two parts. Sheep. Me. This doesn't make sense."

He eased himself down onto the teaching mat and waited for her to join him. Holding up one word at a time he reviewed the story they had learned together. "The Creator made us to have a relationship with him. The dark one deceived us into disobeying the Creator's command. The Creator sent us from the garden to face pain and death. There was only one way back into a relationship with him: a sheep would die instead of me." He waited as she tried to absorb this truth. "But the sheep could not fix the relationship! So the Creator became like a sheep and took our place. He died and we lived. The Way is a person. He is the way back to the Creator."

"I think I need to walk," she said. "If I explain this to the council, they will want to send me away from this garden forever. They will send me into the park, with its wild animals, and I will never be seen again. Only my father, the emperor, can save me now."

Twenty-Three

rdeshir felt surprise at the sensation of a heavy foot pressing down hard in the middle of his back. He had been prostrate on his face, interceding intensely with Yeshua for Lu Hou as she stood before the council. He hadn't heard the guardians slip through his curtain in the pre-dawn hours. Had he fallen asleep?

What would happen to the princess now? What would happen to him?

Before he could react, two guardians pinned his arms behind his back and hoisted him roughly to his feet.

"Stillness is life," the guardian on his left said.

The message was clear: if he remained calm and quiet, he would live—at least for now.

Since he'd been sleeping in his loincloth, they graciously permitted him to slip into his day robe before marching him out into the cool morning. The garden was still and quiet. Even the crickets seemed to have stopped their chirping.

As expected, they took him through the golden gates to the judgment hall. There, Lu Hou stood solemnly within a circle of clay lamps, her hands by her side. She nodded to him as he drew close, but the guardians marched him past her. They stopped within six strides of the council table where the twelve ancient ones sat.

The same old man who had presided before now stood.

"We trust you have rested well," he spoke in Mandarin. "The princess has spent many hours instructing us on all your teaching. It is interesting how you have taken our own script and taught what we ourselves have hardly conceived."

He motioned toward another council member, who handed him a scroll. He took the paper and examined it.

"Every year, the emperor's representative offers a sacrifice of one sheep on the borders to the west in honor of Sheng-Di, the supreme one. The words you speak align with this truth. Our people look in your direction for our origin and our rightness with the supreme one." The man motioned for another scroll to be handed over to him. He scanned the page. "We have copied all the words the princess has given us. You have taught much in these days."

He waited for some time, as though weighing his next words.

Ardeshir motioned for the decision basket. Pulling out one stone at a time, the old man placed them on the table in front of him.

Ardeshir counted. Seven black and five white. Whatever the decision, it was not in his favor.

"You may see us ancients as being unable to change with the time," the old man said. "We have wrestled with the truth we hear. We see where it aligns and where it does not. You are young and may know truth we have forgotten." He pushed the stones forward. "Most of us cannot change enough to accept your understanding of the Way. We have our own way."

A messenger arrived with another scroll and the ancient one accepted it with a slight nod of his head. He unrolled it without expression.

"The emperor grants the union of his daughter to the prince of Persia," he read, keeping his head down. "Together they will face the den of truth. If they survive, they will depart from the garden forever."

The pit in Ardeshir's stomach only deepened at the sound of the princess's wailing. But he kept his eyes trained on the ancient one.

"Do you understand the will of the emperor?" the old man said. "The source of all truth has taken this decision from our hands. Stand before me with the princess and you shall be declared as one. In your union, you will face the pit of lions for three days." He picked up the stones and placed them back in the basket. "This may be a mercy if this God of yours can protect you. No one has survived the lions before, but there is the promise of freedom outside this garden if you do. Now step forward with the princess."

The ceremony was a simple one. Lu Hou stood next to him as erect and still as a statue. One of the ancient ones wrapped a cloth around their wrists and another draped a shawl over their heads. One brought a clay bowl and another poured water over their joined hands.

Still another arrived with a single piece of meat on a plate.

"Eat together," he said.

They did and returned the plate.

A final pair of ancient ones arrived carrying a single goblet into which the other poured rice wine.

"Drink together."

The princess drank first and Ardeshir drank second. They returned the cup.

"Now give your gifts," the first ancient one declared.

Ardeshir had not expected this and hadn't come prepared with a gift. Grappling for an idea, and praying in desperation, he was surprised at his own words.

"I give the princess my whole self, my truth, and the throne of Persia beside my own. I grant her the titles, the honor, and the deference due to such a one who holds that place."

He bowed toward Lu Hou.

"And what do you give?" the ancient one asked, turning to the princess.

Lu Hou pulled her bone flute from her robe. "I have only one thing of value to give. Along with my whole self, I give you this source of joy and hope. Guard it with whatever life we have left."

Ardeshir accepted the flute and then reached for her hand. It was the first time they had connected so intimately. This flute would be their only keepsake from the emperor's garden should they survive the lions.

The ancient one stood at the table, watching them. "I remember my own wedding ceremony. It is a time to remember truth. It is my declaration that you shall have the chance to walk through the gardens for one day before facing the lions."

He sat in his chair.

"The den of the lions will be opened when the sun goes down. Then you shall enter it. After three days, we will extract whatever remains."

The old man reached for another scroll and opened it.

"I did not think I would have to read this scroll, but there are fates beyond our own. We have chosen a new unicorn, a new general to take the place of the one you destroyed." He scanned the words written on the scroll. "These are his words to you: 'The price of fifty horses would have been a small price to gain my loyalty. The terror of the lions will be nothing compared to me if you survive.'"

When the newlyweds emerged from the judgment hall, the sun was already warming the gardens. They walked silently, hand in hand, until they reached the bridge over the koi pond.

"Remember this forever," Ardeshir said to his bride. "It was here that I knew I loved you as a man. It was here that I heard the beauty of your flute. It was here that I promised the true One that I would never leave you, if only he would grant me my heart's desire."

He took the princess in his arms and she rested her head on his shoulder.

"Forget this pond, if you can," she said. "It was here that I lost my dignity when you saved me. It was here that I poured out my sorrow on my flute at the thought of losing you. It was here that I vowed to feed myself to the beasts if I could not spend my life with you."

Ardeshir stepped away and took her chin in his hand. "Why would I want to forget? If we have one day together, it is as good as a lifetime. If we have one moment alone, it is enough to satisfy me forever. If I have one kiss from you, it is all I can hope for."

He kissed her tenderly and they drank of the shared life together that might never be.

The day sped quickly as they shared memories while sitting on the edge of the bridge with their feet dangling just above the water. Once in a while, a familiar face appeared and a quick wave was exchanged.

Just before sundown, Liu arrived and got into the boat the princess had been known to use. He rowed it toward the couple and stopped by the bridge.

"Climb in," he said. "The garden needs to hear one last song from the princess."

From the center of the pond, she stood in the boat and played a haunting melody. Slowly, the shore around the pond came to be lined with observers who drank in the music.

As the sun slid behind the roof of the Red Palace, however, the guardians arrived and waited. Honor demanded that all should be done as the emperor had declared.

From the shore of the pond, the couple waved to everyone and stepped out of the boat. The guardians showed no hesitation. Two of them took Ardeshir by the arms, and the other two flanked Lu Hou. The emperor himself made an appearance as the couple was to be led through the garden toward the forest.

"How far is the lion's den?" Ardeshir asked.

"You will follow the stream that feeds the koi pond. Then you will find it," a guardian answered. "It is a covered pit and we will lower you inside. You may choose which one of you is lowered first."

When they arrived at the lion's den after walking for twenty long minutes, the emperor took his place at the opening. Lu Hou stood before him, a single tear coursing down her cheek and dripping off her chin. The emperor reached for it, then nodded and turned away as the guardians peered down.

The pit was three times the height of a man and would not be easy to escape, even without lions.

"Lower me in first," Ardeshir said.

Lu Hou fell to her knees and sobbed.

He looked down and saw that there were six lions in the low enclosure, five females and one male. The light of the guardians' torches filtered down into the darkness and reflected off the lions' eyes, adding to the terror.

Two of the female cats flicked their tails with unholy curiosity at the new arrivals.

"No fear," Ardeshir said. "My father faced lions. He says that you always face a lion and never show fear. Stand behind me. Yeshua, have mercy on us."

"We can't even see them clearly," the princess said, squinting into the depths of the lion's den. "I never knew lions smelled so bad."

Two of the guardians grabbed Ardeshir, securing a rope under his arms. They kicked his feet out from under him and in moments he was lying flat on the bottom of the pit. A few seconds after that, Lou Hou was lowered more gently to stand beside him.

His skin crawled as he felt warm breath on his hand. One of the lionesses had crept close.

One of the guardians hurled a stone at the male lion and received a roar in return. With that, the emperor and the guardians took up their torches and left Ardeshir and Lou Hou in the dark.

"Stand perfectly still," he whispered.

Lu Hou wrapped her arms around him; her tightening grip only increased the reality of how violently she was shaking.

"Breathe slowly, and remember: the Way is the way. Yeshua is the way. We may meet him now or we may meet him in many years. Dream of the family we shall have when we get to Persia."

Her head rested firmly on the back of his right shoulder and nestled close.

As the minutes passed, her breathing regulated and her grip loosened.

"Maybe she's not hungry," the princess breathed.

"Let's stay quiet and see if they sleep. Yeshua once closed the mouths of lions for an old prophet in my own country. He prayed through the night. I don't know if anyone has lasted three days, though."

"My legs are cramping," she said. "I need to sit down."

"I'll sit with you. Sleep if you can. The more relaxed we are, the easier it will be for them to relax."

The night seemed to last forever, but the first trickles of morning light eventually slipped in through the hole in the roof. Ardeshir hadn't slept a wink. He saw that one of the females had fallen asleep less than a stride away from them. If they had stepped on her in an attempt to create space during the night, their ordeal may already have ended.

The possibility of survival seemed negligible given the prospect of living with the smell, curiosity, and hunger of these lions over three days, but hope flickered deep within him.

Lu Hou rested peacefully with her head on his thigh, and as she stirred Ardeshir strategized about how to draw the lions to himself if the time came. Perhaps if he died, the beasts would allow her to live.

Would it hurt to die this way?

"We still live," she whispered. "I prayed all night for the peace of the Way to live in the heart of the lions."

"Don't stop praying. Four of them are up now… and they're restless." Ardeshir's nose twitched in irritation; the stench of urine grew strong. "Lions need water and food. Do you know how they get such things?"

"Someone feeds them."

Lu Hou rose slowly against the wall. But as two lionesses immediately moved in her direction, she froze in place.

Satisfied, the predators lay down and watched her closely.

"A servant once told me that there is underground water near here," the princess whispered. "It keeps the koi pond fresh."

"One of the old carvers told me the same thing," Ardeshir said. "He said that his grandfather made that pond and filled it by tunneling water from a river near the lion's den. I think my sister and I may have found the source of that river when we first snuck into the palace grounds."

She grabbed his wrist. "The emperor is not the source of all truth. He once told me that no one ever went into the park and came back alive. You are right. Only Yeshua is the Way, the Truth, and the Life."

"We need to get to that water… maybe we can find a way out."

"Why get out? If Yeshua wants to save us, he will save us here."

"I think you believe even more strongly than me," he said, reaching for her hand. "You don't have anything in your pockets to eat, do you?"

She pulled a small bag from her pocket and jingled the coins in it. "This is all I have. I don't think they're edible."

A few moments later, the lions moved toward the middle of the den and looked up toward the hole in the ceiling with some level of expectation.

Ardeshir watched in amazement as he heard scuffling above. Then a small wild pig, secured by a vine, was lowered toward the waiting cats, squirming and squealing. By the time it was within reach, three of the lions balanced on their hind legs and batted their prey.

The pig suddenly dropped and scrambled away from the lions' raking claws, but the well-coordinated pride had it slaughtered and devoured within moments.

One of the beasts looked up for more, but nothing came.

Yawning, the male flumped down onto its side and slept. Meanwhile, one of the lionesses moved toward a dark crease in the wall and disappeared in the shadows. Three others followed.

"I think I know the way to the river," Ardeshir mused.

Lu Hou was stiff with terror. "Did you see what they did to that pig?"

"That's why we don't run and we don't squeal. I think Liu and Yeshua are looking after us."

Twenty-Four

The lions seemed satisfied with the pig, and eventually the male awoke and followed the females down the channel that Ardeshir suspected led to a waterway.

"Maybe we can head down there while they sleep," Ardeshir suggested.

"They will smell us! Then eat us."

In the meantime, they needed to get comfortable and wait. First they relieved themselves in a corner. Then they settled back into their place, all while Lu Hou complained of a sore throat and dry mouth.

The den was cool, although the flies and dust seemed thick. They covered their noses with their sleeves and waited out the long day.

That evening, the lions returned. Apart from a few close bypasses, the pride ignored their two human visitors.

"Keep praying," Ardeshir said.

In the morning, the same routine was repeated, although this time a lamb was attached to the vine and lowered into the den. Lu Hou buried her eyes in Ardeshir's shoulder as the animal was shredded.

When the lions had retreated through the crevice channel, she spoke again. "I remember what you said. The lamb died for our sin. God's lamb died for me. This is truth again."

"You have listened well," Ardeshir said. "One day you will be the master and I will learn again from you. The words which we believe are words of life, not just for learning."

"This truth gives me peace," she said.

Ardeshir rubbed his beard vigorously and changed the subject. "I think these lions are saving us for a time when they don't have enough food. We should leave before that happens. But I made a false assumption. I wonder… do you think the lions are sleeping somewhere else? I think we need to take our chances and get out of here while they're away."

After waiting only a few minutes longer, Ardeshir crept toward the tunnel. The opening was low and they realized they would have to crawl. Seeing that it would be rough on their hands and knees, he tore strips off the bottom of their robes and tied the material around their knees. He then tucked the ragged bottom of their robes up into their belts.

He took one last look into the darkness ahead. If they came face to face with a returning lion while in the middle of the tunnel, there wouldn't be anywhere to escape.

Ardeshir led the way with his new wife behind him.

As they continued down the tunnel, quickly and quietly, the passage grew pitch black. It then took a sharp dip downward and they moved more slowly, forced to reach for handholds to keep themselves from sliding. At one point, Lu Hou lost her grip and slid into him, almost dislodging them both into a tumble. He held his place and waited for her to regain her balance.

This was a steep incline. Perhaps the lions had found another way down to the water.

He heard the lapping of water before he came near it. Still no lions. They rounded a bend, revealing the faint outline of an opening in the rock. Ardeshir also heard the echo of a small waterfall. He almost dropped over the edge of a cliff before realizing they had come to the end of the passage. The river flowed far below.

Where were the lions?

That's when he heard a roar downstream. The lions had likely smelled them.

"I think we found a different path to the river," he said, eyeing the steep drop.

They heard the sound of scrabbling above them as several pebbles cascaded into the water below. The lions must be getting close!

"I think we have to jump and take our chances."

No sooner had he spoken than an avalanche of stone crashed into them, hurling them over the cliffside. While still in midair, Ardeshir drew a quick breath and reached out for Lu Hou—

—and instead caught the raking paw of a falling lion.

The three of them crashed into the water and Ardeshir felt claws rake across his arm as he fought his way toward the surface. He shed his robe quickly and held it in the direction of the panicked beast. Its paw got caught up in the material… but then the lion got swept away with the current.

Moments later, he was headed downstream as well. Suddenly he felt a hand grasp at his foot. He reached down and hauled Lu Hou to the surface. She too had shed her robe.

Ardeshir held her as she coughed, spluttered, and flailed wildly with her arms and legs.

"I have you," he said reassuringly as they floated atop the river. "Be still. We seem to be safe for now."

The current carried them quickly past five lions that had congregated on the edge of the river. They roared as the humans drifted past.

In the distance, Ardeshir detected another roar—the roar of a waterfall.

"Swim to the edge of the river," he said. "The current is getting stronger. We have to hurry."

"I need my robe. No man can see me like this."

"I'm your husband now. It's okay. We will find our robes downstream."

"But you're bleeding," she said, glancing at a cut on his shoulder. "We have to fix that."

"It's just a scratch. We will heal it in the morning."

He pulled her hard toward the edge and soon the two of them clambered out onto a rocky ledge. They sat huddling, finding warmth in each other's arms as the sun went down for another day.

In one more day, they knew the guardians would come looking for them in the den. If they were going to escape honorably, they would have to do it as soon as the sun rose again.

Lu Hou was shy when the sun came up and Ardeshir tried not to stare. They kissed and hid their shyness.

He finally broke away. "We must go down the cliff and follow the river."

"I cannot go like this," she said. "Besides, you are hurt. We need to bind that wound."

"For today, pretend like we're the first man and woman in the garden. Without shame. We'll reach the bottom and find our robes. Then we can escape and create our own garden where no dark ones can live."

She took his hand as they re-entered the water and walked along the shallow edge, following a sheer rockface. The water rushed faster and harder here and they held desperately to the rocky outcropping above their head.

Before long, they came to a ledge where Ardeshir could scramble up. He pulled her behind him until they were safe.

"You have beautiful skin," she remarked.

"And you are beautiful everywhere." He smiled, taking in the view of his wife. "Come, we will climb down the vines. From there, we should be able to find our way back to the garden. I'll go first."

It took all his strength to hold fast to her as they navigated down a steep incline of slippery rock. A steady stream of debris tumbled down along with them and he pitied the effect it had on Lu Hou above.

Their feet finally reached the makings of an animal trail that seemed to follow the path of the river. Dirt, leaves, and twigs nestled in his wife's hair and mud streaked her cheeks.

"I think we need to bathe," he said. "I don't mind if we can't find our robes for a while."

The river here was slow and still, so they entered the cool water to splash and frolic like uninhibited children; it seemed to wash away more than the dirt and debris. He helped wash out her hair and tenderly rubbed her scalp as she floated.

When he found his robe still wrapped around the paw of the deceased lion, she shredded the fabric and used it to bind his wound. In the pocket, she found her bone flute, still unbroken. She wrapped it carefully, happy for the touch of home.

He offered her his robe to wear, but she sprang away into the water and swam downstream.

"I'll find my own," she said. "Until then, I may wander the garden without shame."

She found her robe caught on a tree branch a fair distance downstream. With relief, she slipped it around her body as the sun blazed high overhead.

"Someone will see us in the river soon," she said. "It would be good to dry ourselves and our clothes. A teacher told me many years ago that the emperor's river eventually flows into the great river where many people fish. We may soon be forced to leave the emperor's land."

She reached into her robe and found there the pouch of coins, undisturbed. She shook the bag with a smile on her face and then sat to watch the water flow by.

"Husband, are you now glad that you observed me as a man observes a woman?"

He knelt beside her. "I could not be happier."

"Then kiss me."

The first drops of rain spattered and a cool breeze whispered over them as they awoke in each other's arms. They dipped quickly in the river and then donned their robes with a small sense of regret. The tumbling dark clouds overhead foretold a heavy storm.

"We need to find a cave for shelter," he said.

"Don't make it one with lions." She smiled. "I need to eat soon."

They found some berry bushes, but the few handfuls they harvested only served to stimulate more hunger pains.

"We should have seen people by now," Ardeshir noted. "The emperor's realm can't be this large. We've seen birds and small animals, but it seems like nothing big lives around here. The guardians will be checking on the lions soon, though, so we need to find a horse."

A short time later, they found their way blocked by a tall stone wall. They worked their way alongside it until Lu Hou spotted a column of smoke spiraling into the sky.

"Fire," she said.

Moments later, three men carrying snared rabbits walked off a side trail and stopped to stare at them.

"Hello," said the tallest of the three. "Welcome. Who are you and what brings you to our village? You look like you're in trouble."

Lu Hou nodded. "Thank you for welcoming us to your village. We are a husband and wife who are lost. We need to find a horse so we can travel to our destination."

"Come with us," the man replied. "Are you hurt? Your husband doesn't look like he's from around here."

"Yes, he was hurt," Lu Hou said as they fell into step with the men. "He is from Persia. He has been of great service to the emperor, but we've completed our time here."

"Does he not speak?" the man asked.

"I speak," Ardeshir replied in Mandarin. "I simply love to hear my wife's voice."

The village did have a horse, fortunately, though it cost two of the coins in Lu Hou's pouch. Both sides celebrated the value of the deal.

Another coin purchased a new set of untattered robes for the newlyweds.

After a large meal, having heard they were close to the great river, husband and wife mounted their newly acquired horse and sauntered away from the village, continuing to follow the wall.

Their journey downriver lasted two more days, when they came to a metropolis with more people than either of them had ever seen before. The docks boasted storehouses of trade from such locales as Egypt, Rome, Persia, and Hindustan. An endless stream of laborers hauled freight from ships to the docks, and then from the docks to carts.

Lu Hou was fascinated by the Roman glassware on display by merchants who carefully loaded the fragile valuables destined for inland settlements. Woven baskets filled with Arab and Hindustani spices piled next to wooden chests of gold guarded by fierce soldiers daring anyone to come close. Scents of rose, jasmine, cinnamon, vanilla, honey, licorice, oregano, olive oil, frankincense, and myrrh betrayed the presence of perfume vials in the mix.

Being loaded on ships destined west were bales of silk, jade, carvings, pottery, and other items of food. Crates of silk robes and clothing joined this endless train of goods.

A broad-chested Egyptian sidled up to the duo as they ogled all the activity. He tried communicating several languages before Ardeshir understood his Persian: "Are you traders looking for passage, or pirates in need of plunder?"

Ardeshir nodded enthusiastically. "Yes, we are. Passengers, that is. My wife and I need to get to Persia."

The Egyptian smiled and grasped Ardeshir by the wrists. "I can show you to my captain, who can take you most of the way. But you'll need to find some warm clothes to survive at sea."

After spending some time in the market and meeting the energetic Hindustani captain of the man's ship, husband and wife finally settled onto the burgeoning deck of a broad two-storied freighter with its sails already unfurled.

"We sail tonight," the captain told them. "Our cabins are full, so you'll have to find a place on deck. I have leather blankets with which you can shelter when you need."

He motioned to another Hindustani sailor who brought a large covering and dropped it at their feet before scrambling up the mast.

Lu Hou watched the man in wide-eyed amazement. "He's like a monkey!"

Ardeshir squeezed her shoulder as he started unravelling the leather blanket near a pile of crates that had been lashed together. By anchoring the blanket to the top of the pile, stretching it out at an angle, and arranging a few crates to secure the bottom, he was able to create a comfortable space for both of them.

Lu Hou, the princess who had never been outside the emperor's palace and garden, took it all in with astonishment.

"Won't the sea swallow us?" she asked. "My servants once told me that the great sea contains dragons that swallow great ships like this."

Ardeshir led her to the railing where they could continue to watch the bustle of activity ashore. "This is an adventure you'll never forget. It may also be one you never want to repeat."

By the end of the first week, Ardeshir became certain that they would never be able to complete this journey by ship. Lu Hou had spent every day at the railing retching. She'd grown pale, thin, and angry. The sailors looked at him knowingly but kept to their tasks.

"Storms coming soon," the captain advised him as he passed one morning. "We've had good sailing until now, but you might want to put her feet on land for a time. I'll return one of your coins so you can find a place to stay."

It was another two days before they arrived at a port.

Twenty-Five

Once Lu Hou had slept an entire day at an inn, Ardeshir couldn't convince her to try boarding another ship.

"I would rather walk to the end of the world than feel my stomach crawl out of my mouth again," she pleaded.

The ship's captain had not returned the coin he promised, however, and the ship had departed before dawn without waiting to see whether they would return.

In the days that followed, the sense of intimacy and trust between the couple faded. But Ardeshir did coax his new wife to visit the market and sample the delicacies.

"Walking to Persia could take us half a year or more," he explained, "and there are bandits who would kill us simply for our robes."

"What kind of a people do you live among?" she asked. "Barbarians?"

"One of the sailors told me we have sailed from Wu to Hainan in the south. Your father's lands are large. It took us eleven days by ship to get here. It would take fifty-five days to go this far by camel."

The dialect of the people had some overlap with Mandarin, but their ability to communicate with the locals had deteriorated to little more than gestures and hand signals.

"I want to go home," the princess said in despair.

"We are going home," Ardeshir said. "Remember, your own father disowned you and banished you from the garden. We only have each other now."

She wept for the better part of the day, then stiffened, shook her head, and gave him a weak smile. "The Way is the way. You told me the truth. I still have my flute."

With stern determination, she marched to the marketplace and played her flute. She set a bowl before her and passersby dropped small coins, bits of fruit, and odd trinkets into it.

She returned to the inn that evening with new purchases and, more importantly, new pride in herself.

Ardeshir located a trader who needed a driver for his second donkey cart on a caravan heading west. The group would meet up with others along the way before reaching Hindustan.

As they moved inland and reached the Silk Road, the number of larger caravans, mounted troops, pilgrims, and curiosity seekers grew more frequent. Lu Hou took a new interest in the diversity of people, landscapes, animals, and clothing styles on display—and even the foods being consumed in the villages they passed.

Four weeks along, Lu Hou stood beside Ardeshir in the light of the full moon staring at the towering peaks of the Himalayas.

"Never in my life did I imagine how far you travelled to get me," she said. "Never did I realize how hard the journey could be. Now that I have seen your sacrifice, I am ready to be your wife again." She kissed him quickly on the cheek and blushed. "Are we almost home?"

Ardeshir pulled her close. "My sweet lotus blossom, we have all the time in the world to get home. And it will take us at least two months to get there. Play your flute along the way to keep everyone around us joyful. The time will go faster."

She lay her head on his shoulder. "I miss seeing dragons…"

He glanced at her in surprise.

"Oh! My family is called the descendants of dragons," she explained as she unwound her hair and let it fall to her waist. "The dragon has a fierce head, an ox horn, the body of a snake, fish scales, and an eagle's claws. Together, they demonstrate the power of humans. At one time, only the emperor had a dragon on his robe. The ministers wore the snake. Civil officials wore birds; the crane was most important, then the pheasant, peacock, lark, quail and others."

She stood back and eyed his expression of curiosity.

"In my kingdom, we know who others are by what they wear. But in this world, no one knows who others are. There are unicorns, lions, leopards, tigers, bears, rhinoceroses, seahorses…" She shook her head in confusion. "Back home, the general was the only one in the kingdom to wear the unicorn and you killed him."

Ardeshir held her tight as she released all she had known through tears.

Having taken this route three times already, Ardeshir could anticipate the upcoming challenges and spectacles. His pleasure doubled with Lu Hou's enthusiasm and settled as her flute calmed his nerves and the temperament of those in their vicinity. The multiethnic mix of travelers shared smiles freely as they gathered around fires each evening to listen to the ancient melodies of the east.

A young woman, about Lu Hou's age, showed a special fascination for the flute and Lu Hou began to give her lessons as they travelled. While many of the young woman's early attempts made her listeners wince, they did create the luxury of extra personal space for the couple around their cart.

When the caravan prepared for river crossings, the outriders responsible for security established sentries and organized the caravan into small pods to ferry across. Bandits twice probed the caravan's safety measures with quick ambushes, but they were repelled with few losses. After each success, the traders grew more confident.

Ardeshir purchased a leather tarp in a village they came through and fashioned a rounded covering so he and Lu Hou could have some privacy when needed. This improved his wife's mood tremendously.

By the time the remnants of the original caravan reached the borders of Persia, Ardeshir was tempted to trade their accumulated wealth for a horse and strike out on their own. The prospect of returning to the pressures and responsibilities of the farm no longer pulled at him, and he felt no desire to take the throne. Without his father to impress, he felt tired and wanted to ease his bride into a more peaceful life.

For three days, he debated his next steps.

Finally he approached a cart driver who had already bartered away much of his supply of jade and silk for spices and precious gems.

"My wife and I live close by and we will be leaving soon," the driver said to Ardeshir. "I would ask you to count our coin and use it to find a new driver to take over our cart."

With the coin, Ardeshir bought a horse and another leather tarp. He and Lu Hou then headed out into the wilderness for a week, following a quiet stream whose course he knew. It gave the couple a chance to replay their first days as husband and wife, back when there had been no shame between them.

One night by their fire, he asked Lu Hou to play her flute.

"The flute is gone," she said. "I gave it to the woman so she could learn. I am no longer with the Han. I am Persian ."

Lu Hou chattered fluently now in Persian and responded well to his lessons of history and geography as he named mountains, rivers, streams, and valleys.

As they crossed the Zagros mountains, passed Susa, and took the road that would eventually lead them to the farm, he looked up and detected a dark plume of smoke curling into the sky ahead of them.

Ardeshir urged their mount forward—and when they arrived, his worst fears were realized. Where the farm should have been, smoldering piles of ash and charcoal lay heaped and neglected. Not a soul was in view.

The only bit of color attached to the gate was a red flag with a golden dragon waving in the breeze.

The Han dragon, the personal symbol of the emperor himself, had come to claim them at the farthest reaches of their world. Now they truly only had each other, and there was no garden in which they could share their love.

"We must move further west to find your garden," Lu Hou said. "The Way is the way. As long as we are together, we are home. Now you are my prince and I am your princess."

About the Author

Jack A. Taylor (PhD) grounds his novels in solid historical research and real-life characters. His eighteen years in Kenya, current work in Rwanda, and twenty-five years in cross-cultural ministry keep him globally aware and connected. He and his wife Gayle live outside Vancouver, Canada and have been married for forty-seven years. They have four children and eleven grandchildren. Jack is an award-winning author with Faithwriters and writes monthly for Light Magazine and other publications (www.jackataylor.com). He has helped found nine organizations, including the New Hope Community Services Society, which has provided housing for more than eight hundred fifty refugees from sixty countries. He is a credentialed marriage coach and focuses on helping leadership couples when he isn't writing (www.1heartcoaching.com). He has master's degrees in leadership, counseling, and theology, plus his PhD in counseling. Jack's hobbies include raising tropical fish and reading.

One Last Wave

Katrina [Katie] Joy Delancey has staked her life on keeping the past and future away from her heart. But she is no master of fate or captain of her own journey. A near fatal race with a wild stallion, an unexpected discovery of lost African journals, and a chance encounter with a tae kwon do master, leads Katie through love, grief, faith and terror like she's never known it.

One Last Wave is a story about being discovered by faith and love no matter where you are, no matter where you've been, and no matter what you think may lie ahead.

No Place to Run

Pushed to her limits, Katie Delancey stands at the pinnacle of a bridge. Growing up as a missionary kid changes nothing now. Witness protection has failed her. The determined human trafficking ring has tracked her down. A continent away from her fiancé, she is wooed by a 'wolf in sheep's clothing' and trapped. Weary and vulnerable from losing her mother to cancer, the upcoming wedding of her sister, the loss of her horse, the needs of the refugees she loves, and the constant surveillance of the police, she has no place to run. When you haven't got a prayer where do you turn? Katie is about to find out.

No Place to Run is the second novel in an adventure about rediscovering faith, hope and love when the maze of life seems to close all exits. It is a story about how the whispers of the past can be keys to our future. It is a tale about how the illusions of the obvious may be sinister traps designed to destroy us.

Stretching for Home

A blissful love nest amidst a brutal Minnesota winter turns into a fiery ordeal of grief and terror as Katie is caught up in the never-ending pursuit of human traffickers who want to eliminate her from their deadly game. Isolated and forced to go undercover with the RCMP, the gambit almost backfires. Escaping to Africa doesn't release her from the trail of death relentlessly pursuing her.

Stretching for Home is an education into the heart of missionary kids searching for healing as life tumbles in around them. Their quest for home can be as elusive as a rainbow's pot of gold. Finding old roots and spreading new wings can be a challenge.

The Cross Maker

First-century Palestine is a hotbed of political, cultural, and religious intrigue. Caleb ben Samson, a carpenter from Nazareth, and Sestus Aurelius, a Roman centurion, both want peace. Can this unlikely partnership accomplish what nothing else has accomplished before? Can they bring about peace through the power of the cross? And what role will Caleb's childhood friend Yeshi play in a land that longs for hope?

In *The Cross Maker*, Jack Taylor weaves a tapestry of creative history, powerful characters, and dynamic dialogue to bring to life a shadowy world. In a land where tragedy is as common as dust, triumph is about to make itself known.

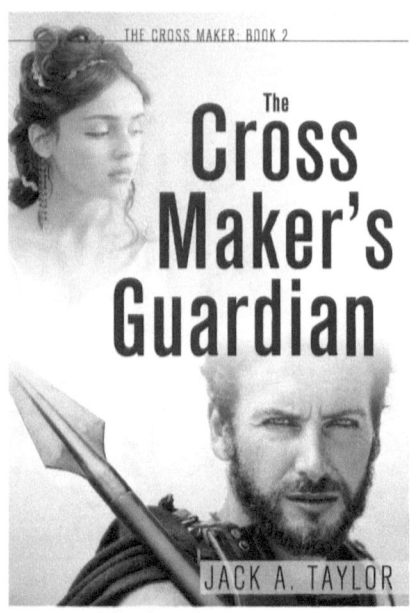

The Cross Maker's Guardian

Roman legions thunder across first-century Palestine, seeking to use the power of the cross to crush the lightning strikes of the zealots led by Barabbas. Behind the scenes, a secret squad of thespian assassins are being trained—and Titius Marcus Julianus is caught up in this silent whirlwind, conscripted to be the new guardian of the cross maker, Caleb ben Samson.

Titius is fuelled by vengeance and love as he seeks to regain his stolen Roman estate and the young Jewish slave who once captured his heart. Meanwhile, voices from his past and present wrestle for control of his heart and mind.

In *The Cross Maker's Guardian*, Jack A. Taylor unveils the clash between the Roman and Jewish civilizations as they battle for life in a world suffused with international intrigue. Descriptive narrative, biblical history, and powerful characters all come alive in this thrilling read where death and love are only a blink away.

The Cross Maker's Champion

Persian slaves who fight for their lives in gladiator arenas rarely rise to be any-one's champion. But the wounded Nabonidus is soon wooed by two women—a priestess at the Temple of Artemis and a humble follower of Yeshua, Daphne. Soon he must learn the truth about himself—is he a missing Persian prince or simply an unwanted orphan?

The arena claims whatever soul may venture there, and Demetrius, a silver-smith, joins forces with a giant German giant gladiator, Selsus, to confront the followers of the Way.

Meanwhile, Caleb, Suzanna, Titius, and Abigail fight through their own life-threatening challenges to join the apostle John and Nabonidus in time. Soon the arena will be packed with chanting patrons. Who will still remain standing when the final blood is spilt?

Jack A. Taylor weaves his readers through a maze of Ephesian mysticism and terror as Roman and pagan powers combine to destroy the infant movement of the Way before it takes its first steps out of its birthplace.

Honest Conversations on Thriving through Conflict

When Ministry and Marriage Collide

Over twenty-five percent of marriages among today's ministry leaders face significant struggle and strain. The demands and temptations of our public and private worlds often create a tension that pushes our love relationships to the breaking point. Through honest conversations with seven couples, Jack A. Taylor reveals five quagmires that can capture the souls of dedicated leaders.

Areas like Identity, Attachment, Calling, Family, and Intimacy can seem straightforward until you're stuck in the challenges they present. *When Ministry and Marriage Collide* provides over fifty practical tools to help strugglers move from striving to thriving. Ideally, this work is designed to be paired with a relationship coach (see 1heartcoaching.com), but it is sufficient on its own to produce significant conversations with anyone willing to delve into the roots of their challenges.

Based on crucial training from the Thriving Relationship Center, readers will discover the five stages of thriving relationship growth and six foundational pillars for healthy intimacy and communication. After the vows—in the middle of real life—investing in your most important earthly relationship is vital to avoid becoming another statistic. While the couples described here are fictional composites, the issues they deal with are anything but imaginary.

The Sacrifice

The Temple of Jerusalem was recognized as one of the seven wonders of the ancient world, but how did it rise out of the rubble of social chaos, international intrigue, family mutiny, and a passionate quest for the Messiah?

How did two simple servants of Yahweh linger through bloodshed and traumatic leadership changes to remain standing when the day of the Messiah's arrival finally came?

In a place dedicated to sacrifice, there was one sacrifice no one expected. This is the untold story of the years before the event that forever changed the course of world history.

www.ingramcontent.com/pod-product-compliance
Lightning Source LLC
Chambersburg PA
CBHW022158260626
47155CB00019B/3332